FEB 2007

DATE DUE

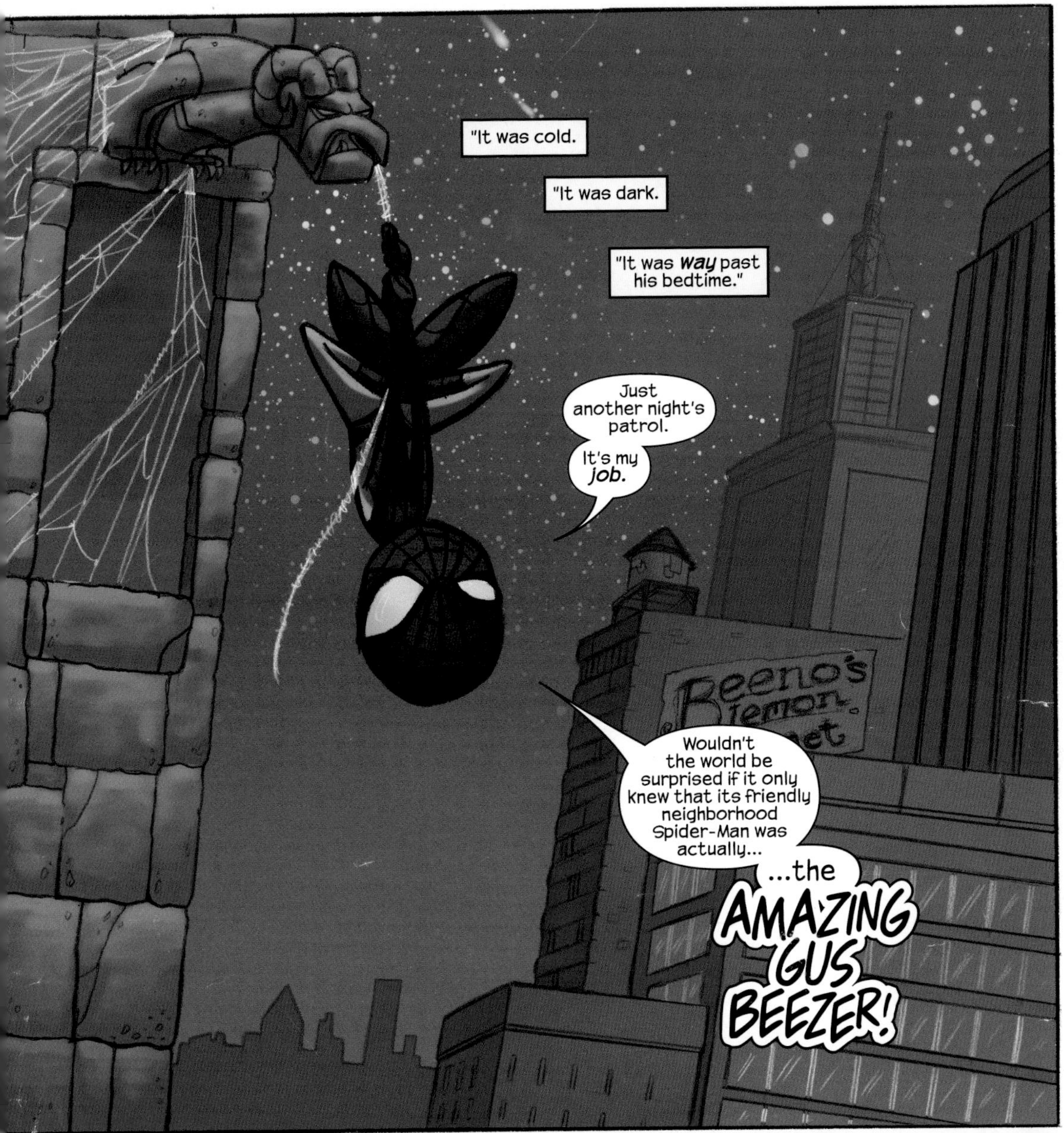
"It was cold.
"It was dark.
"It was *way* past his bedtime."
Just another night's patrol.
It's my *job.*
Beeno's
Wouldn't the world be surprised if it only knew that its friendly neighborhood Spider-Man was actually...
...the
AMAZING GUS BEEZER!

"GREEN GOBLIN" GAIL SIMONE
Spider-Script
JASON "THE LIZARD" LETHCOE
Arachnid-Art
HI "FLYING" FI
Spectacular-Colors
DAVE "SUPER" SHARPE
Web-Letters
MIKE RAICHT
Editor
JOE QUESADA
Editor in Chief
DAN BUCKLEY
Publisher

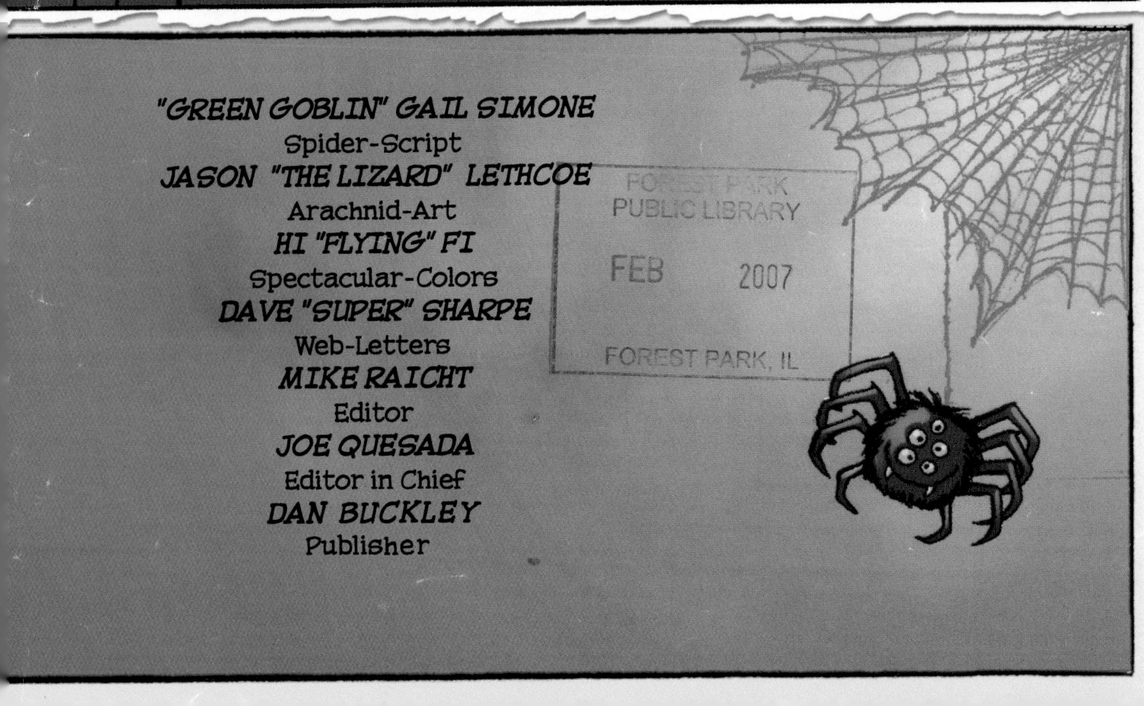

VISIT US AT
www.abdopub.com

Spotlight, a division of ABDO Publishing Company Inc., is the school and library distributor of the Marvel Entertainment books.

Library bound edition © 2006

Library of Congress Cataloging-in-Publication Data

Gus Beezer With Spider-Man

ISBN 1-59961-047-7   (Reinforced Library Bound Edition)

All Spotlight books are reinforced library binding and manufactured in the United States of America

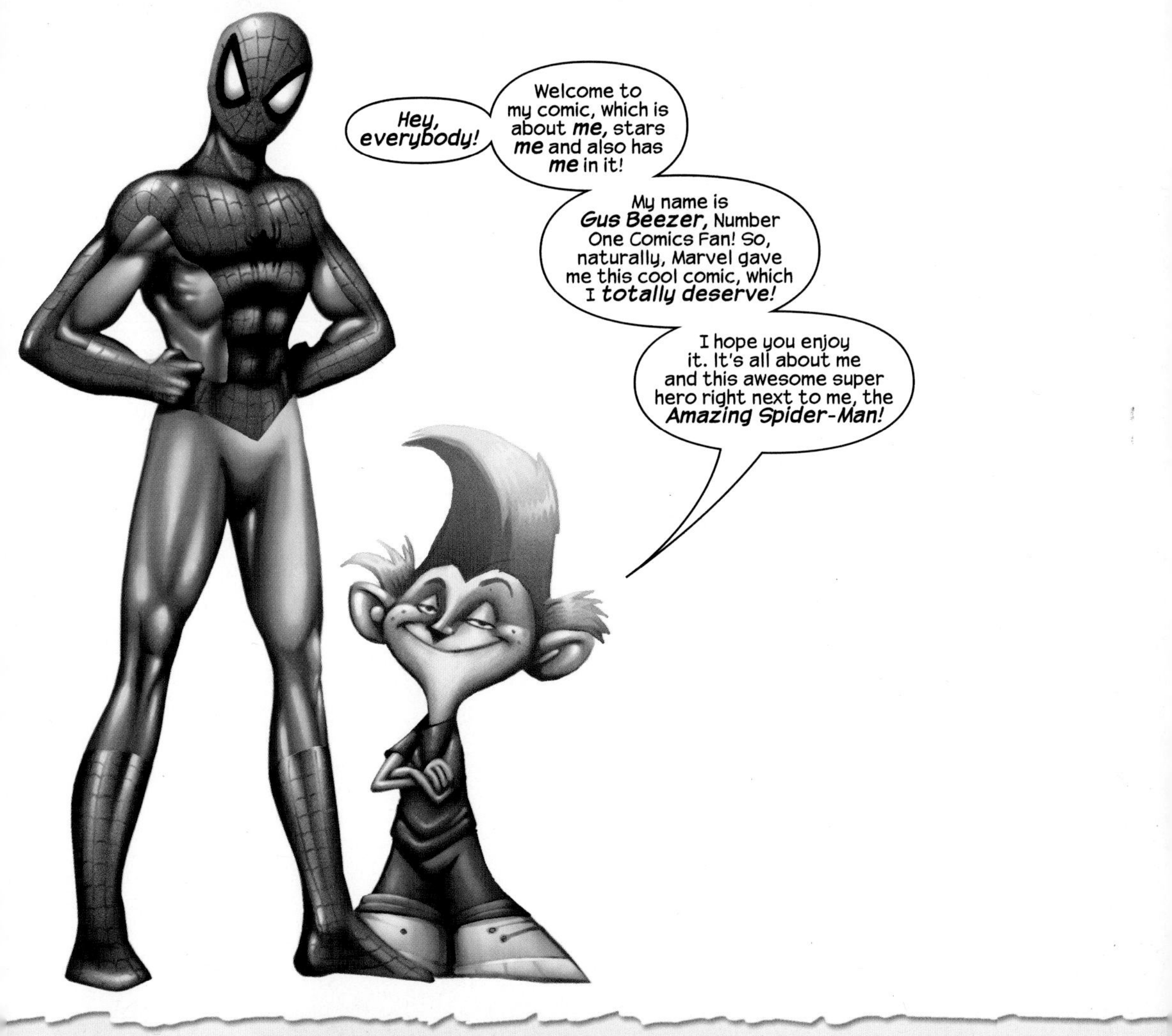
Hey, everybody!
Welcome to my comic, which is about me, stars me and also has me in it!
My name is Gus Beezer, Number One Comics Fan! So, naturally, Marvel gave me this cool comic, which I totally deserve!
I hope you enjoy it. It's all about me and this awesome super hero right next to me, the Amazing Spider-Man!

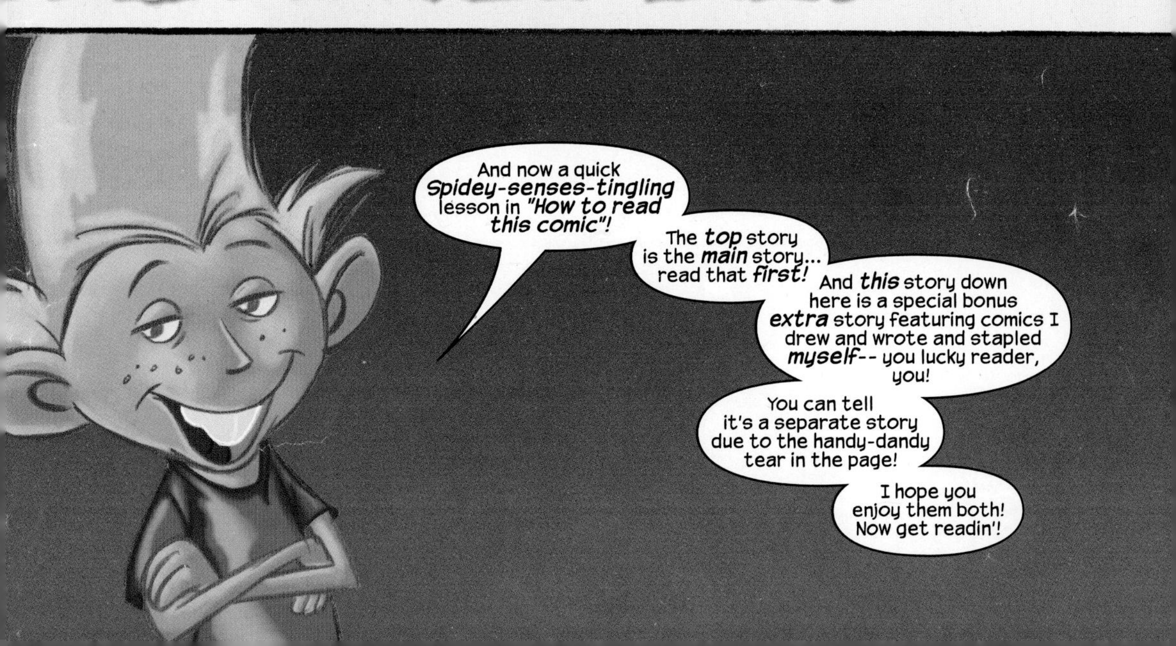
And now a quick Spidey-senses-tingling lesson in "How to read this comic"!
The top story is the main story... read that first!
And this story down here is a special bonus extra story featuring comics I drew and wrote and stapled myself-- you lucky reader, you!
You can tell it's a separate story due to the handy-dandy tear in the page!
I hope you enjoy them both! Now get readin'!

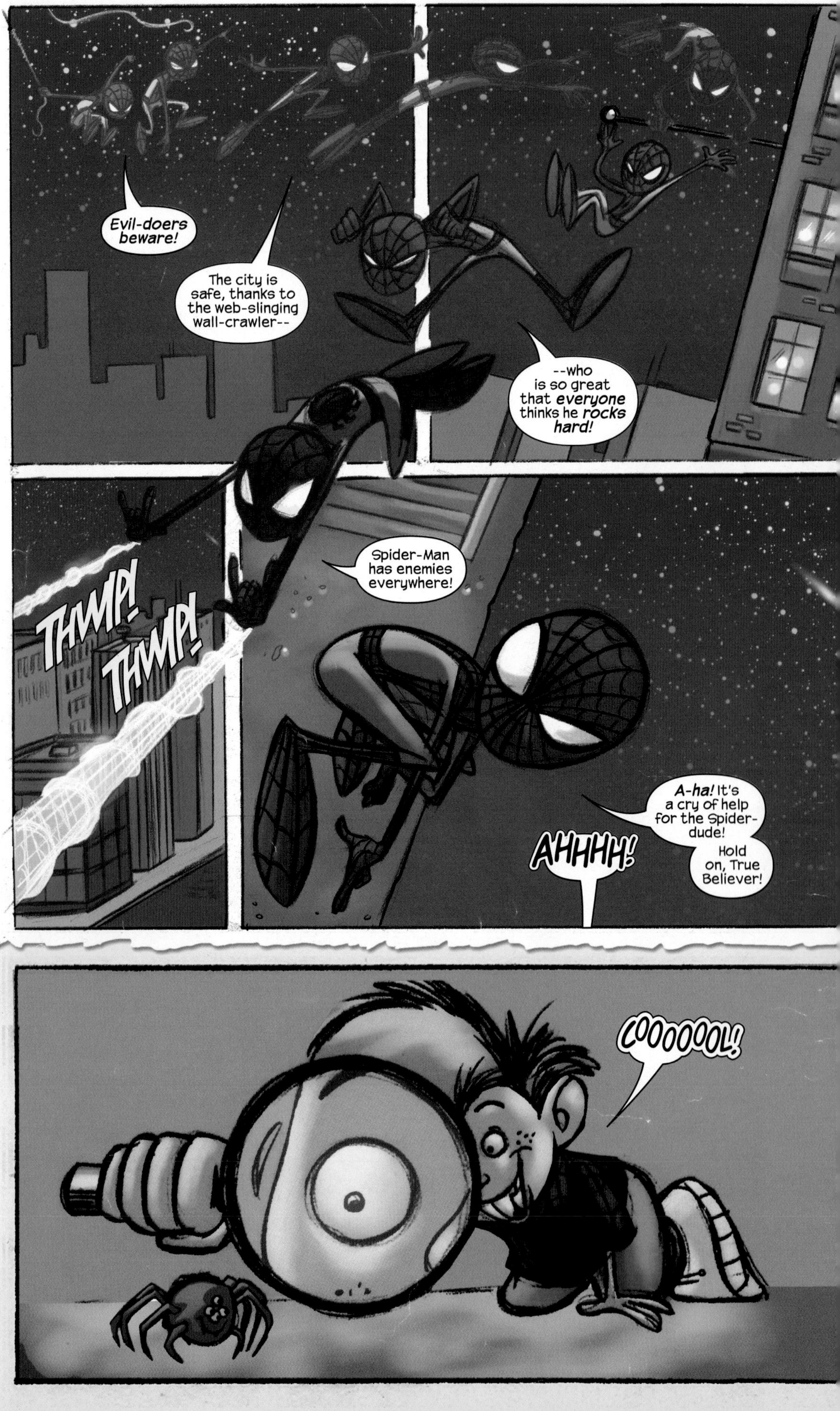

Evil-doers beware!
The city is safe, thanks to the web-slinging wall-crawler--
--who is so great that *everyone* thinks he *rocks hard!*
THWIP! THWIP!
Spider-Man has enemies everywhere!
AHHHH!
A-ha! It's a cry of help for the Spider-dude!
Hold on, True Believer!
COOOOOOL!

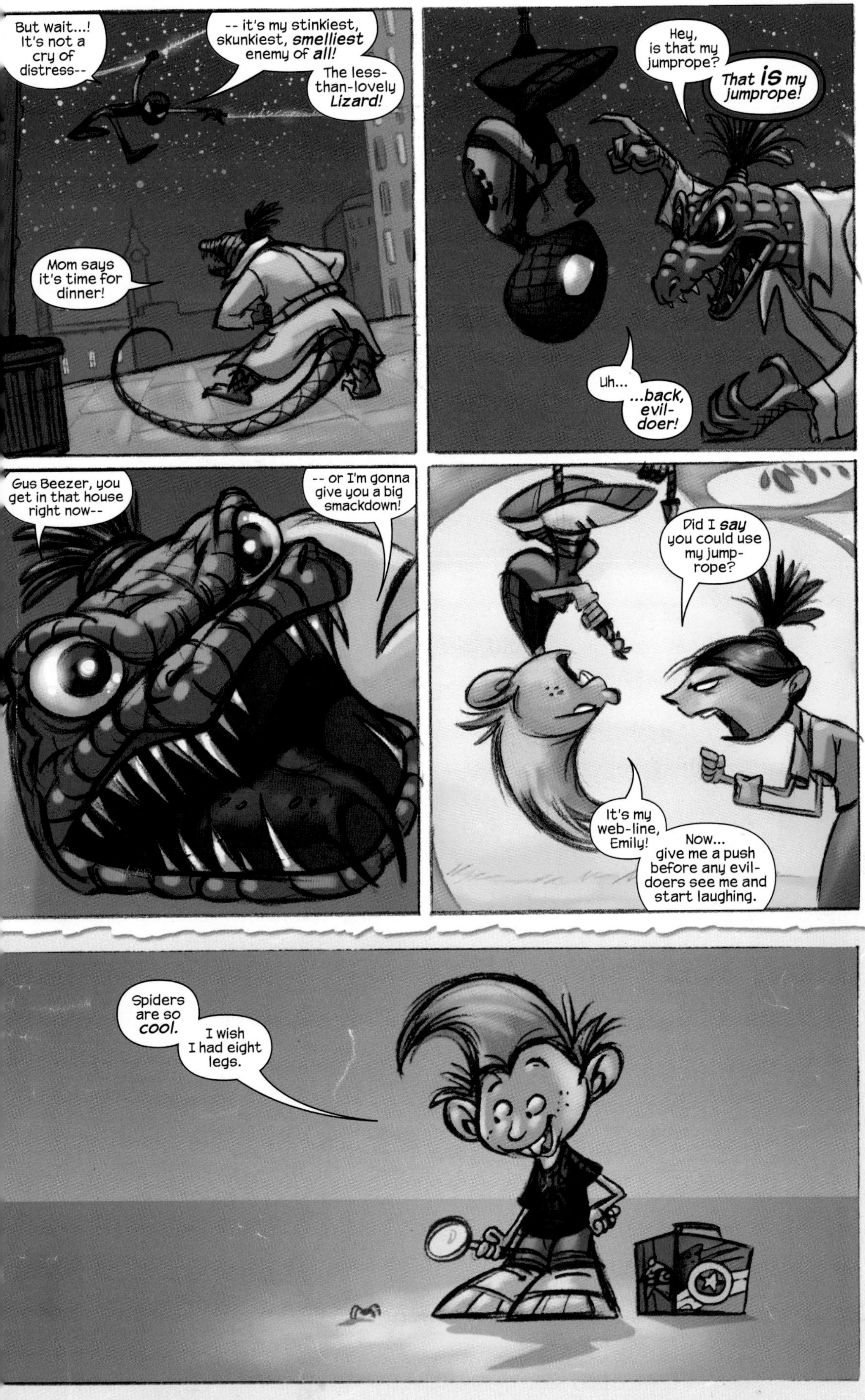

But wait...! It's not a cry of distress--
-- it's my stinkiest, skunkiest, *smelliest* enemy of *all!*
The less-than-lovely *Lizard!*
Mom says it's time for dinner!
Hey, is that my jumprope?
That **IS** my jumprope!
Uh...
...*back, evil-doer!*
Gus Beezer, you get in that house right now--
-- or I'm gonna give you a big smackdown!
Did I *say* you could use my jump-rope?
It's my web-line, Emily!
Now... give me a push before any evil-doers see me and start laughing.
Spiders are so *cool.*
I wish I had eight legs.

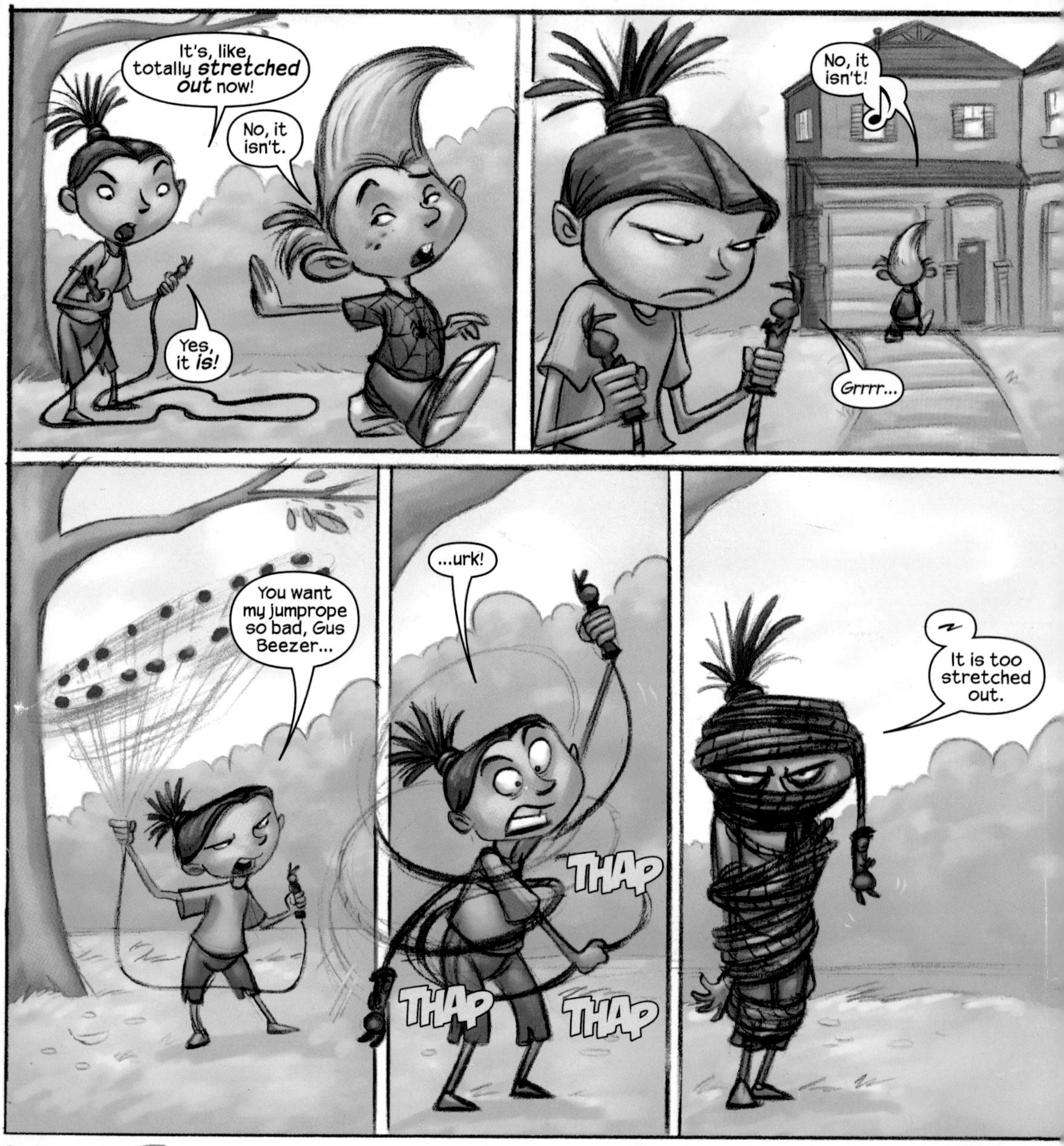
It's, like, totally stretched out now!
No, it isn't.
Yes, it is!
No, it isn't!
Grrrr...
You want my jumprope so bad, Gus Beezer...
...urk!
THAP
THAP
THAP
It is too stretched out.

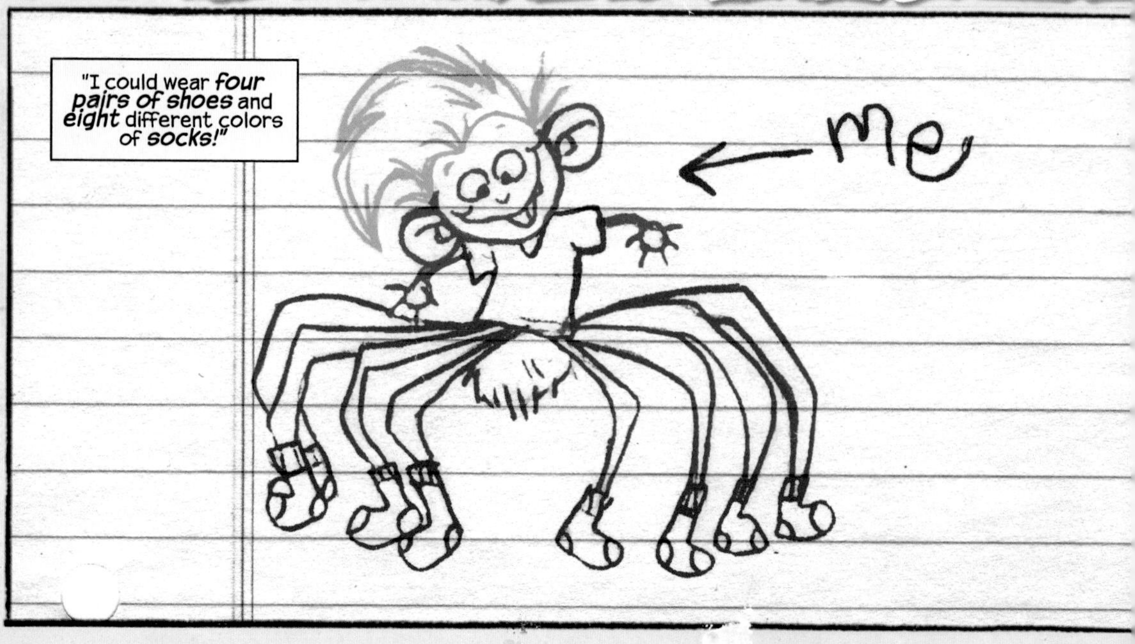
"I could wear four pairs of shoes and eight different colors of socks!"
me

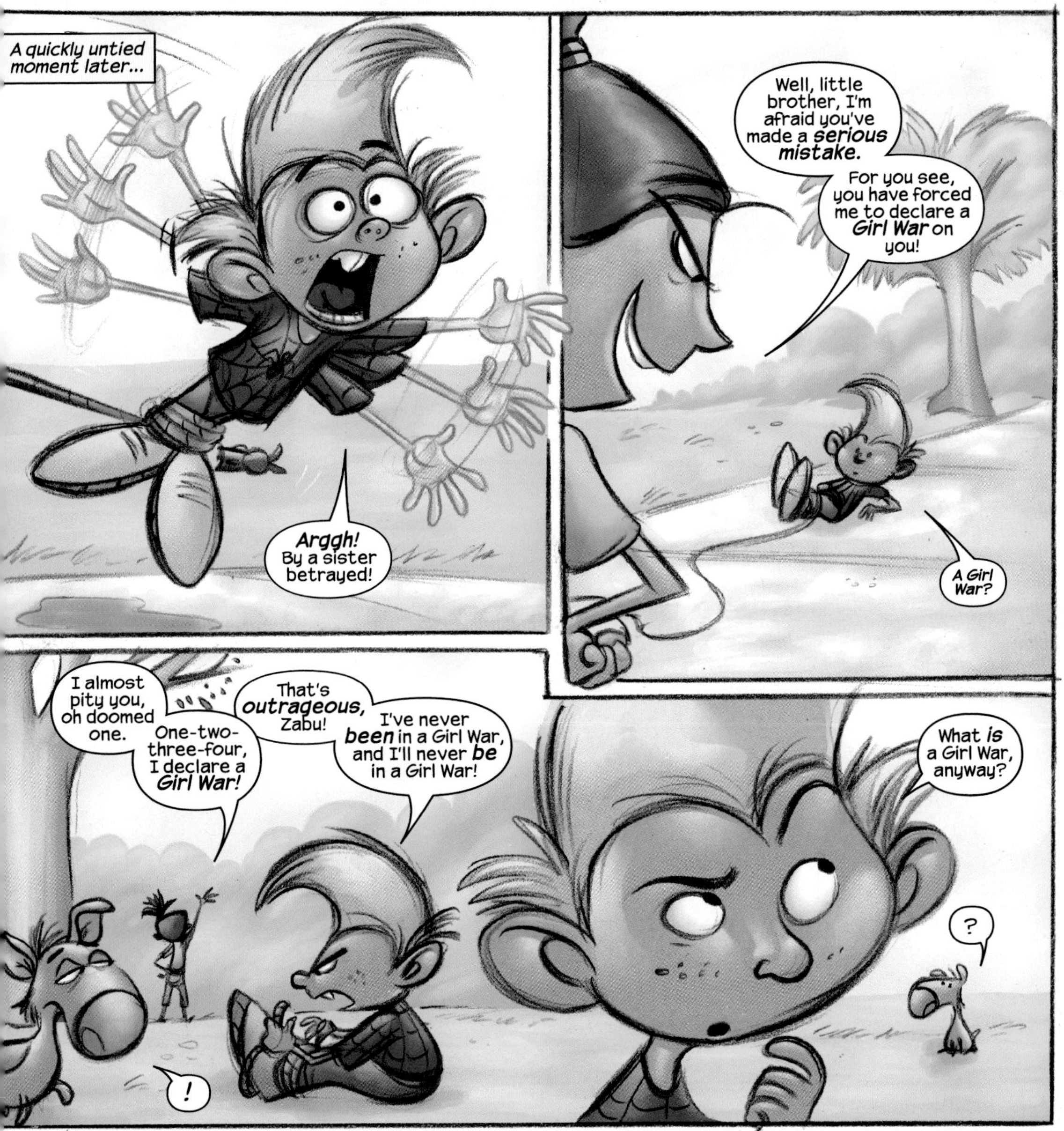

A quickly untied moment later...
Argh! By a sister betrayed!
Well, little brother, I'm afraid you've made a serious mistake.
For you see, you have forced me to declare a Girl War on you!
A Girl War?
I almost pity you, oh doomed one.
One-two-three-four, I declare a Girl War!
That's outrageous, Zabu!
I've never been in a Girl War, and I'll never be in a Girl War!
!
What is a Girl War, anyway?
?

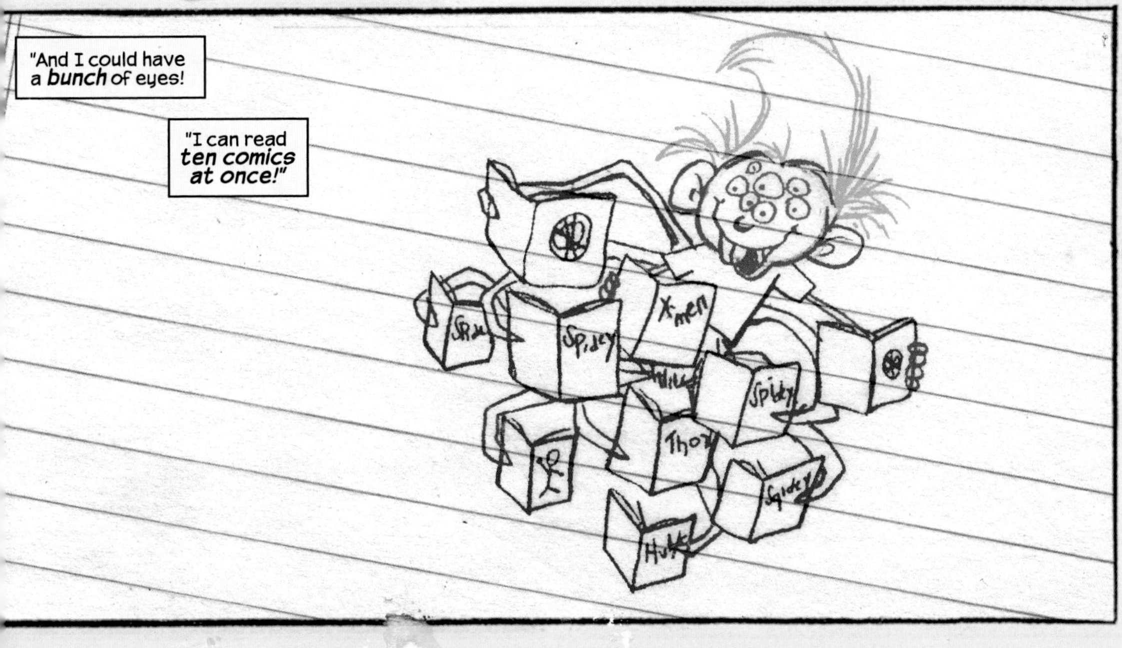

"And I could have a bunch of eyes!
"I can read ten comics at once!"
Spidey
X-men
Spidey
Spidey
Thor
Spidey
Hulk

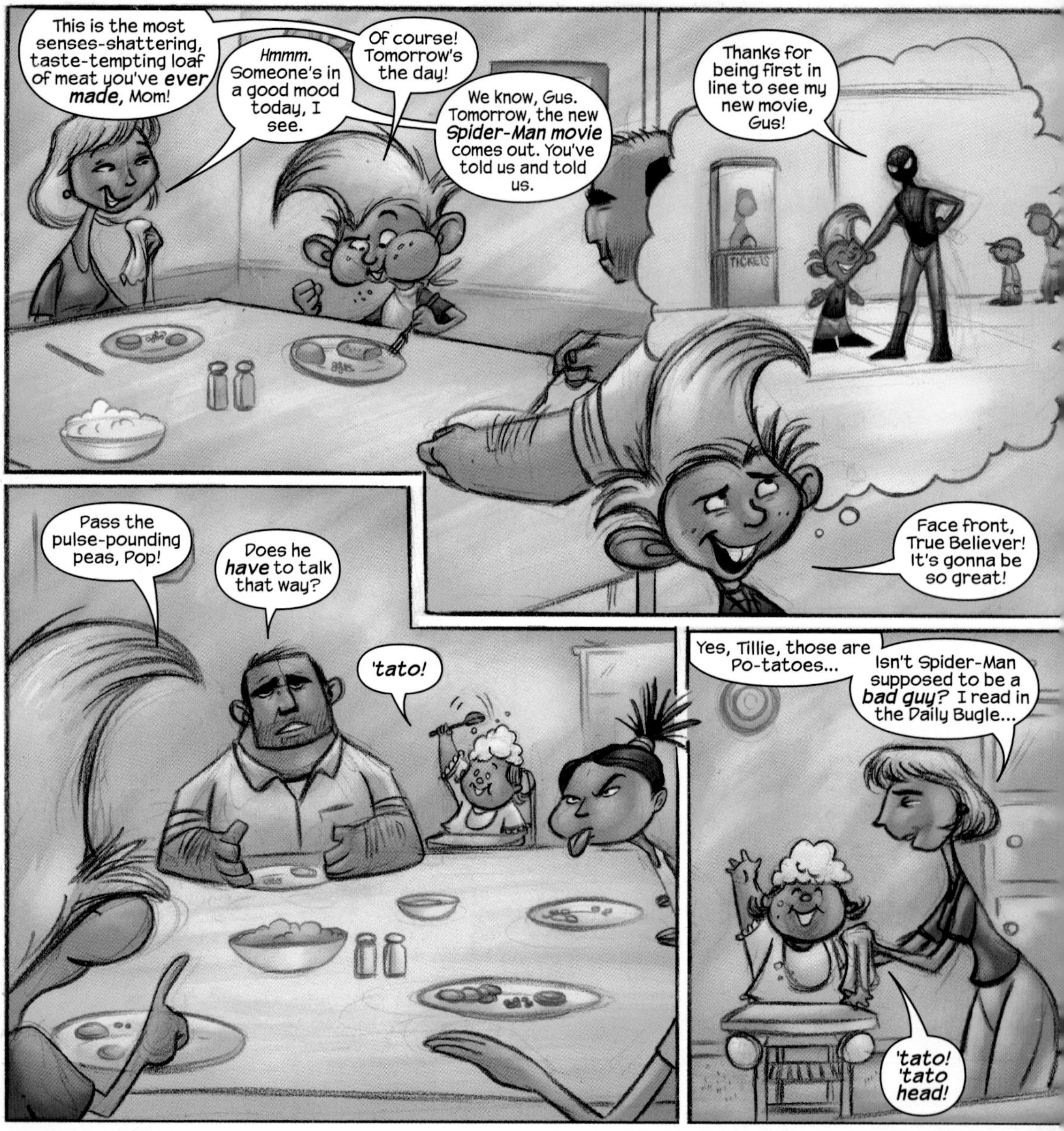
This is the most senses-shattering, taste-tempting loaf of meat you've *ever made,* Mom!
Hmmm. Someone's in a good mood today, I see.
Of course! Tomorrow's the day!
We know, Gus. Tomorrow, the new ***Spider-Man movie*** comes out. You've told us and told us.
Thanks for being first in line to see my new movie, Gus!
TICKETS
Face front, True Believer! It's gonna be so great!
Pass the pulse-pounding peas, Pop!
Does he ***have*** to talk that way?
'tato!
Yes, Tillie, those are Po-tatoes...
Isn't Spider-Man supposed to be a ***bad guy?*** I read in the Daily Bugle...
'tato! 'tato head!

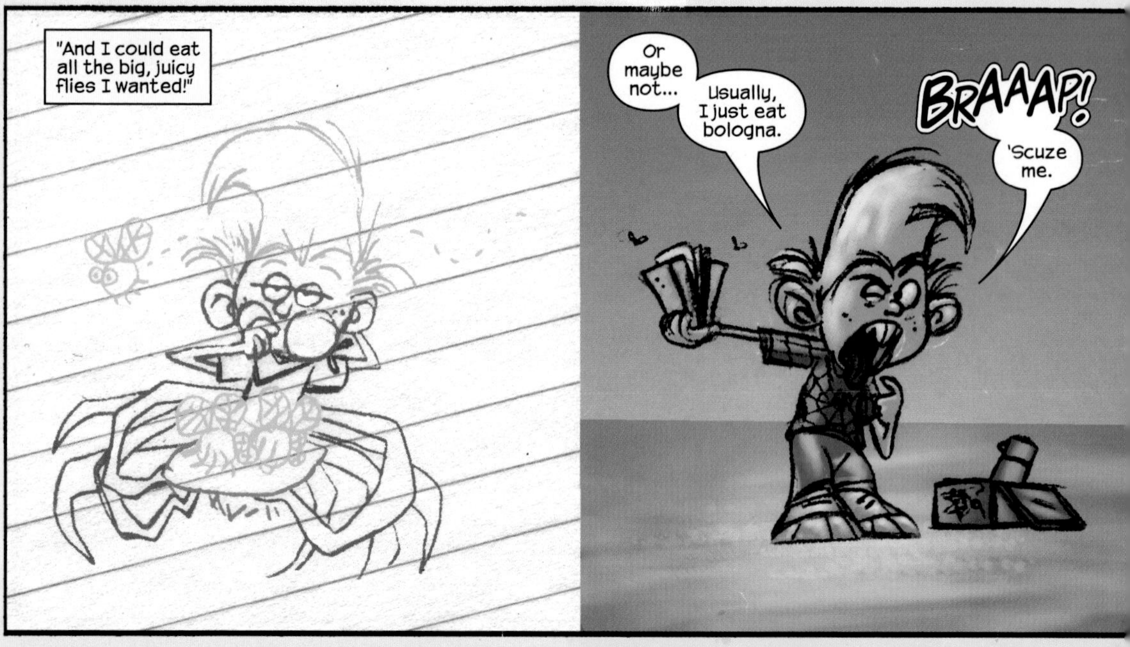
"And I could eat all the big, juicy flies I wanted!"
Or maybe not...
Usually, I just eat bologna.
BRAAAP!
'Scuze me.

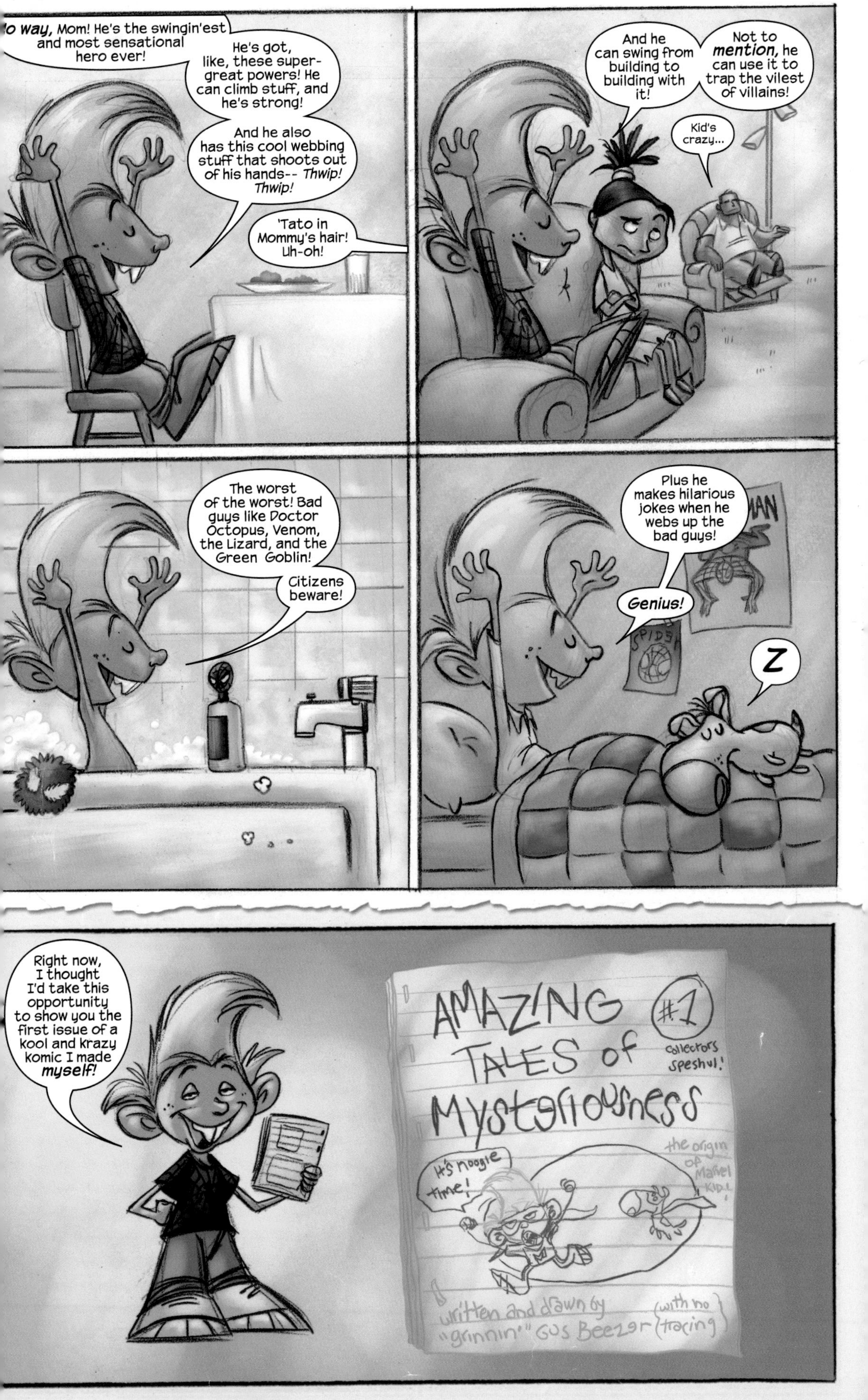

o way, Mom! He's the swingin'est and most sensational hero ever!
He's got, like, these super-great powers! He can climb stuff, and he's strong!
And he also has this cool webbing stuff that shoots out of his hands-- *Thwip! Thwip!*
'Tato in Mommy's hair! Uh-oh!
And he can swing from building to building with it!
Not to *mention,* he can use it to trap the vilest of villains!
Kid's crazy...
The worst of the worst! Bad guys like Doctor Octopus, Venom, the Lizard, and the Green Goblin!
Citizens beware!
Plus he makes hilarious jokes when he webs up the bad guys!
Genius!
Z
Right now, I thought I'd take this opportunity to show you the first issue of a kool and krazy komic I made *myself!*
AMAZING TALES of Mysteriousness
#1
collectors speshul!
the origin of Marvel Kid!
It's noogie time!
written and drawn by "grinnin'" Gus Beezer
(with no tracing)

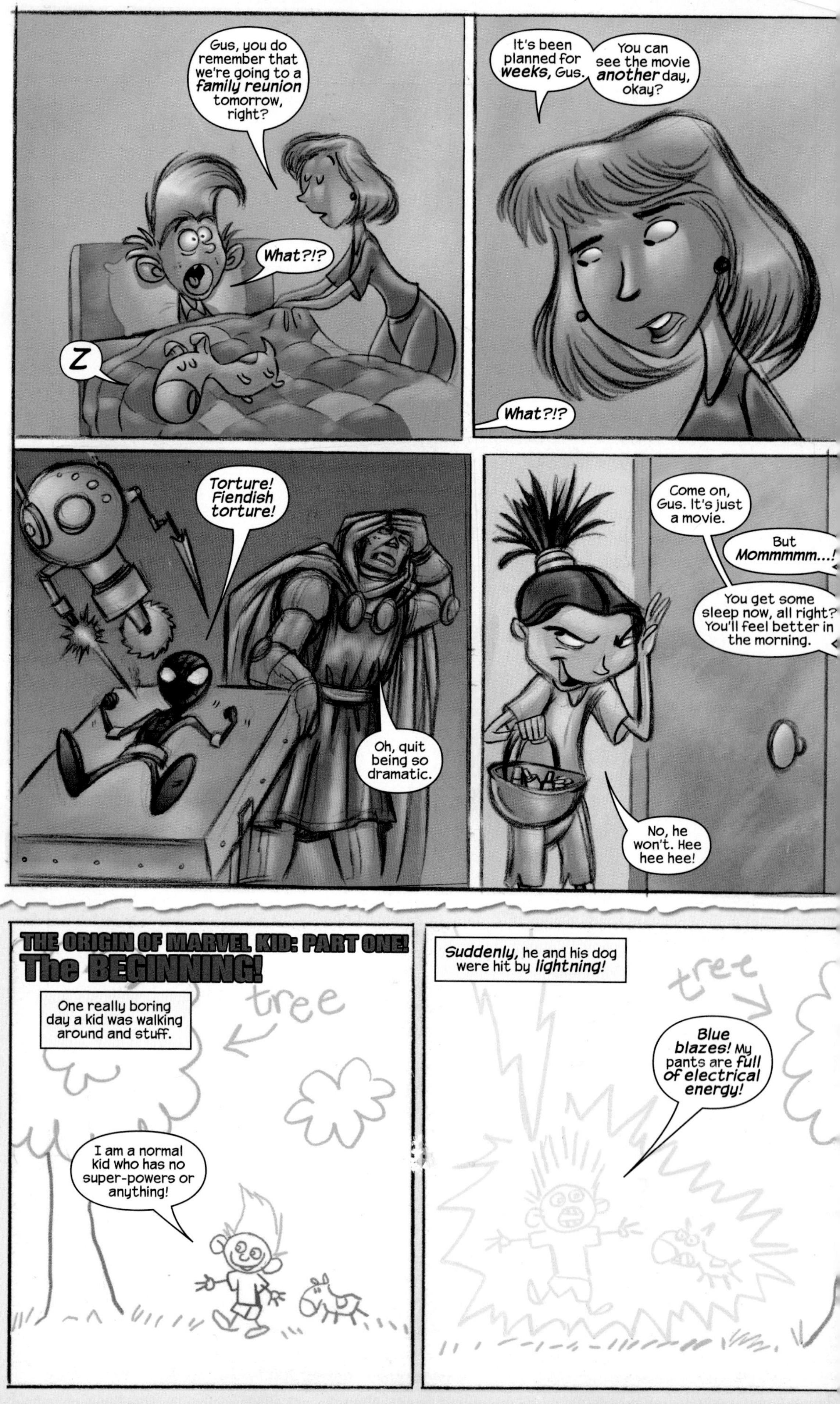

Gus, you do remember that we're going to a *family reunion* tomorrow, right?
What?!?
Z
It's been planned for *weeks*, Gus.
You can see the movie *another* day, okay?
What?!?
Torture! Fiendish torture!
Oh, quit being so dramatic.
Come on, Gus. It's just a movie.
But *Mommmmm...!*
You get some sleep now, all right? You'll feel better in the morning.
No, he won't. Hee hee hee!
THE ORIGIN OF MARVEL KID: PART ONE!
The BEGINNING!
One really boring day a kid was walking around and stuff.
tree
I am a normal kid who has no super-powers or anything!
Suddenly, he and his dog were hit by *lightning!*
tree
Blue blazes! My pants are *full of electrical energy!*

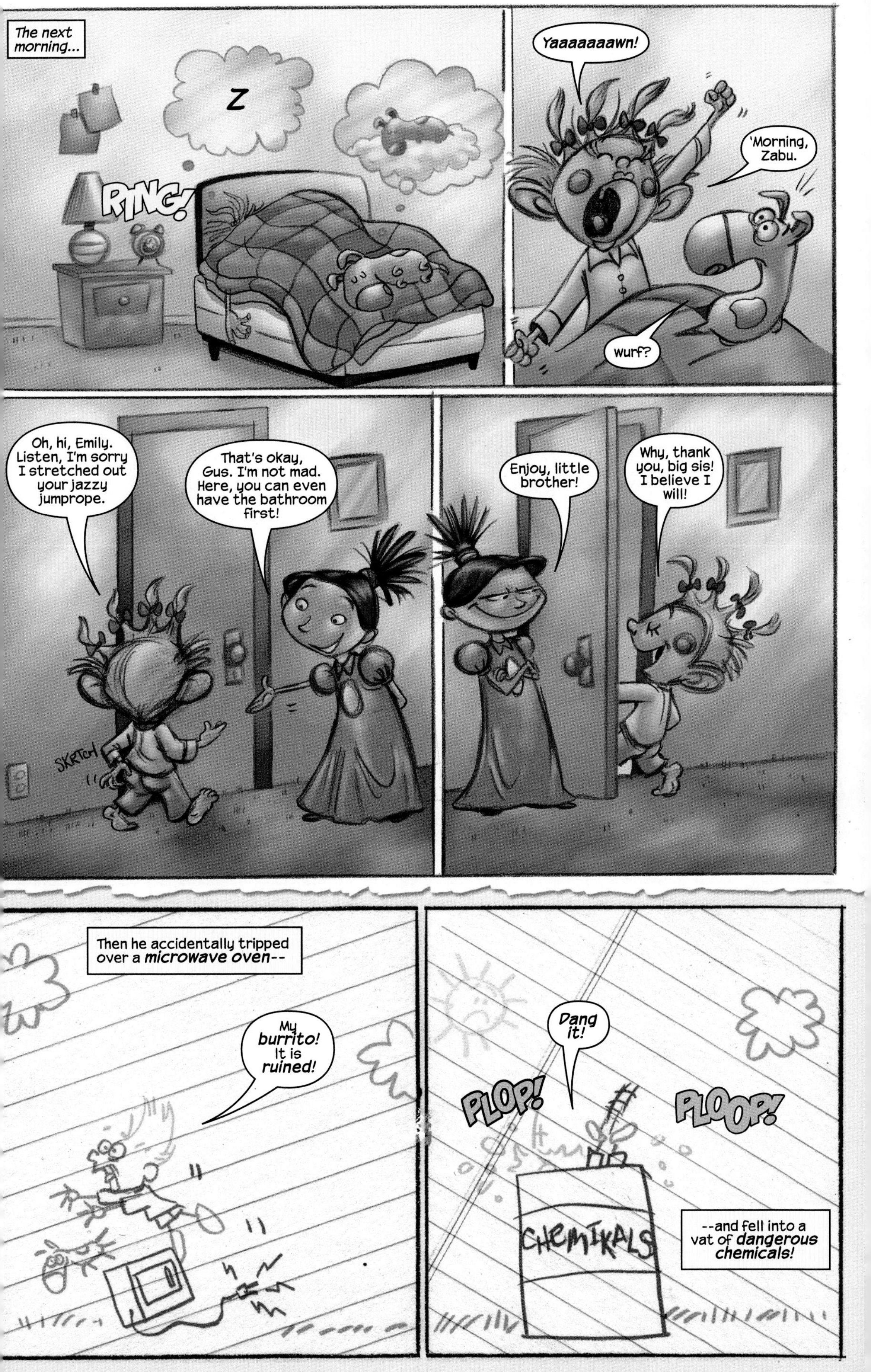
The next morning...
Z
RING!
Yaaaaaaawn!
'Morning, Zabu.
wurf?
Oh, hi, Emily. Listen, I'm sorry I stretched out your jazzy jumprope.
That's okay, Gus. I'm not mad. Here, you can even have the bathroom first!
SKRTCH
Enjoy, little brother!
Why, thank you, big sis! I believe I will!
Then he accidentally tripped over a microwave oven--
My burrito! It is ruined!
Dang it!
PLOP!
PLOOP!
CHEMIKALS
--and fell into a vat of dangerous chemicals!

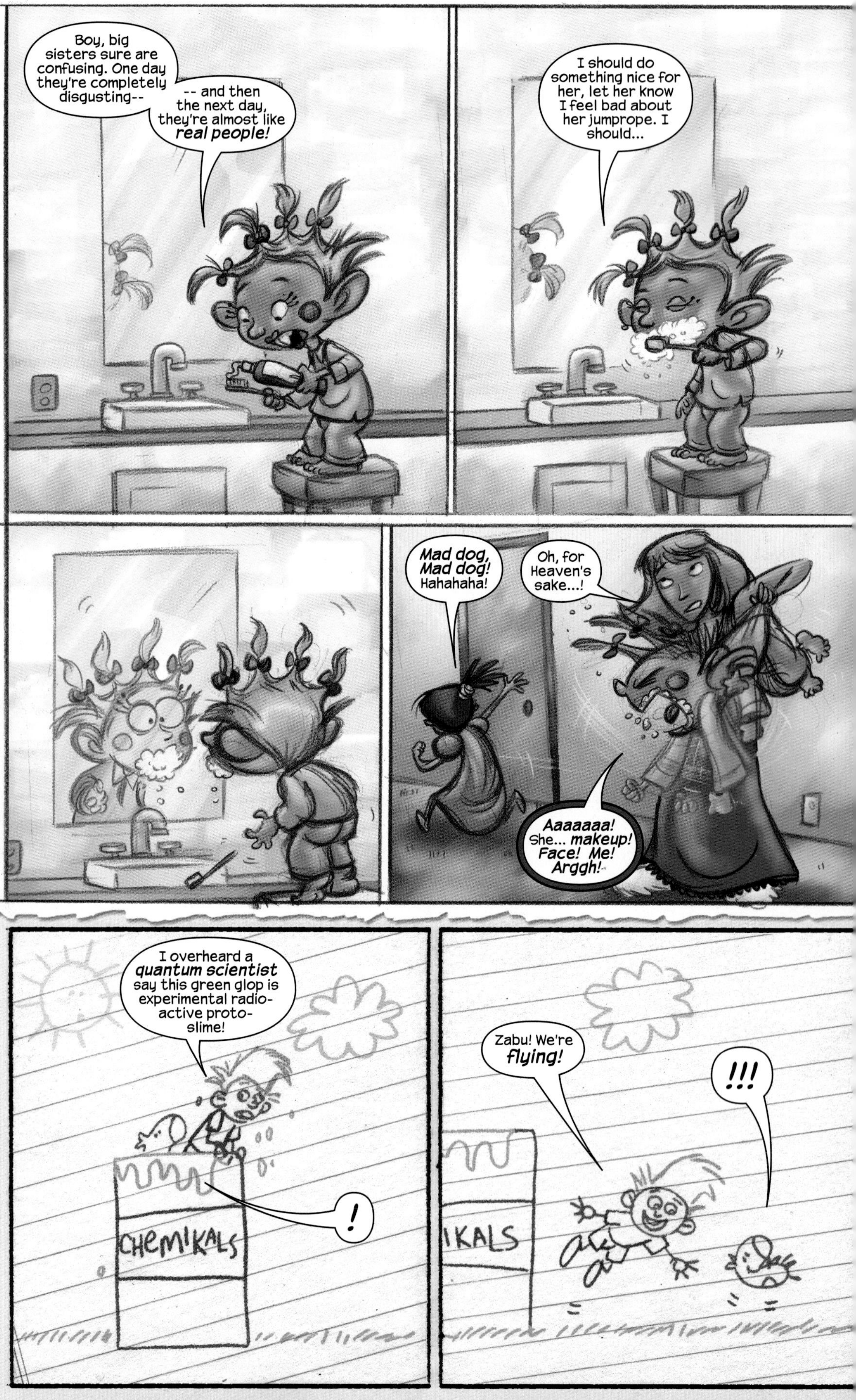
Boy, big sisters sure are confusing. One day they're completely disgusting--
-- and then the next day, they're almost like *real people!*
I should do something nice for her, let her know I feel bad about her jumprope. I should...
Mad dog, Mad dog! Hahahaha!
Oh, for Heaven's sake...!
Aaaaaaa! She... *makeup!* *Face! Me! Arggh!*
I overheard a *quantum scientist* say this green glop is experimental radio-active proto-slime!
!
CHEMIKALS
Zabu! We're *flying!*
!!!
IKALS

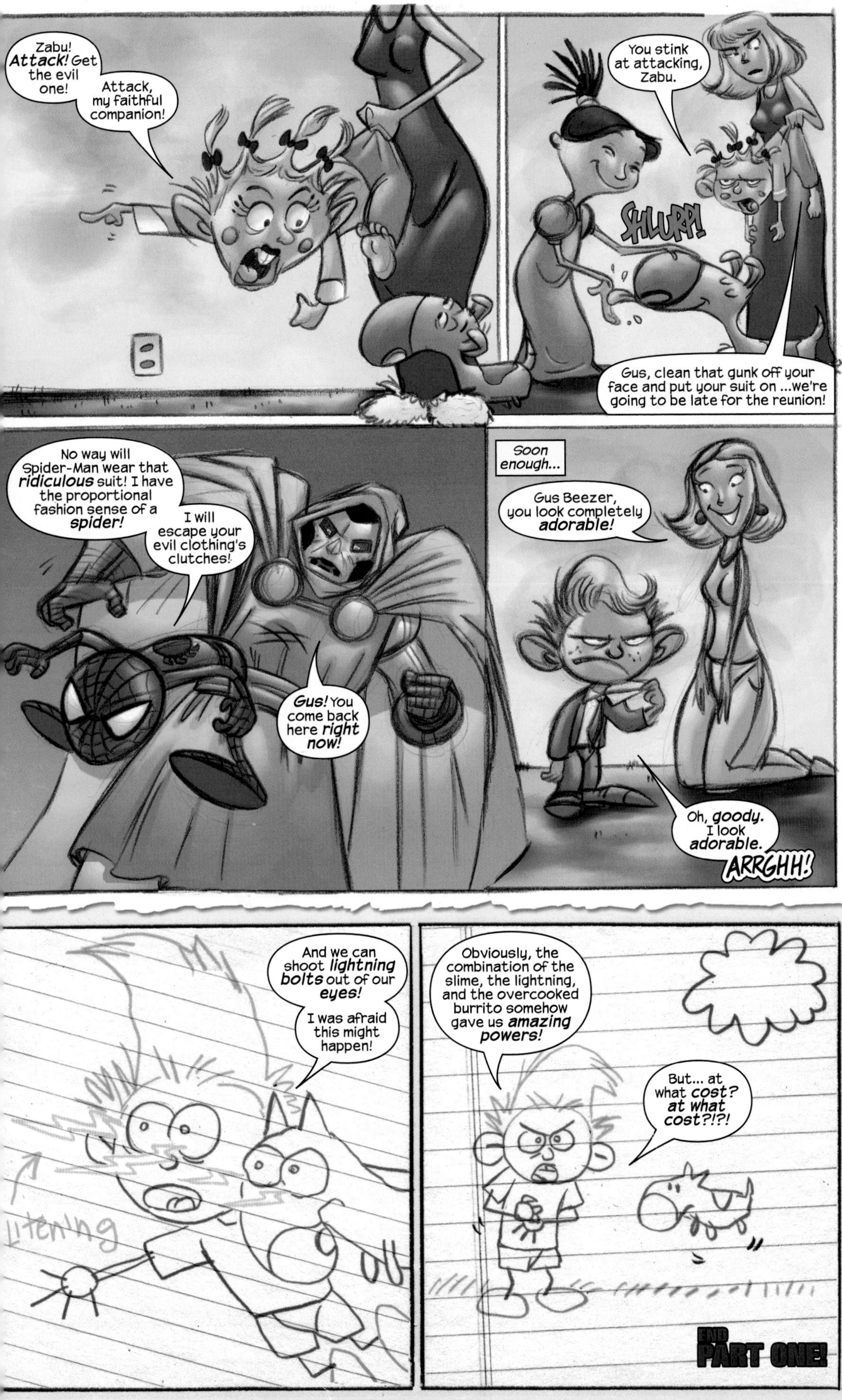

Zabu! Attack! Get the evil one!
Attack, my faithful companion!
You stink at attacking, Zabu.
SHLURP!
Gus, clean that gunk off your face and put your suit on ...we're going to be late for the reunion!
No way will Spider-Man wear that ridiculous suit! I have the proportional fashion sense of a spider!
I will escape your evil clothing's clutches!
Gus! You come back here right now!
Soon enough...
Gus Beezer, you look completely adorable!
Oh, goody. I look adorable.
ARRGHH!
And we can shoot lightning bolts out of our eyes!
I was afraid this might happen!
litening
Obviously, the combination of the slime, the lightning, and the overcooked burrito somehow gave us amazing powers!
But... at what cost? at what cost?!?!
END PART ONE!

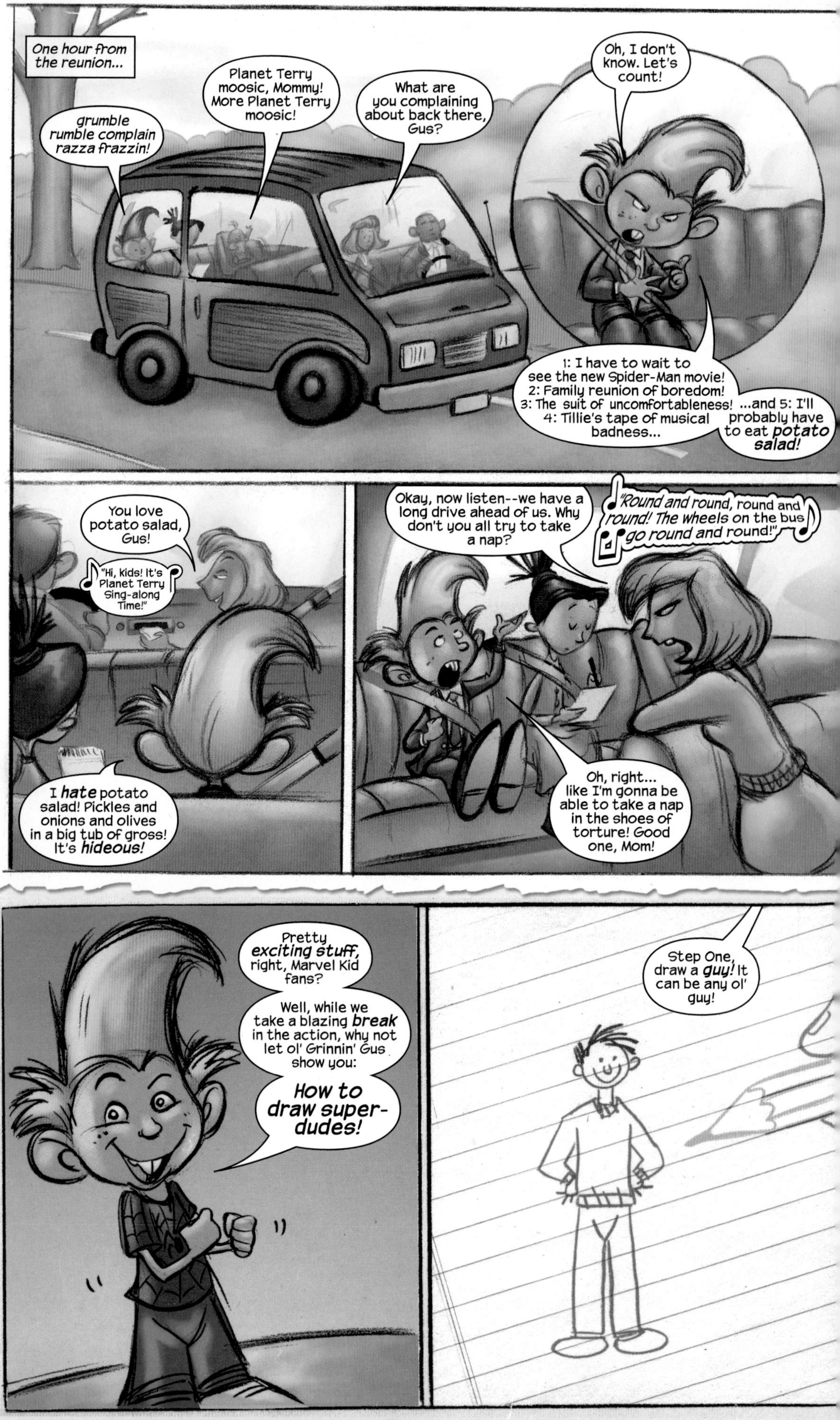
One hour from the reunion...
grumble rumble complain razza frazzin!
Planet Terry moosic, Mommy! More Planet Terry moosic!
What are you complaining about back there, Gus?
Oh, I don't know. Let's count!
1: I have to wait to see the new Spider-Man movie! 2: Family reunion of boredom! 3: The suit of uncomfortableness! 4: Tillie's tape of musical badness...
...and 5: I'll probably have to eat potato salad!
You love potato salad, Gus!
"Hi, kids! It's Planet Terry Sing-along Time!"
I hate potato salad! Pickles and onions and olives in a big tub of gross! It's hideous!
Okay, now listen--we have a long drive ahead of us. Why don't you all try to take a nap?
"Round and round, round and round! The wheels on the bus go round and round!"
Oh, right... like I'm gonna be able to take a nap in the shoes of torture! Good one, Mom!
Pretty exciting stuff, right, Marvel Kid fans?
Well, while we take a blazing break in the action, why not let ol' Grinnin' Gus show you:
How to draw super-dudes!
Step One, draw a guy! It can be any ol' guy!

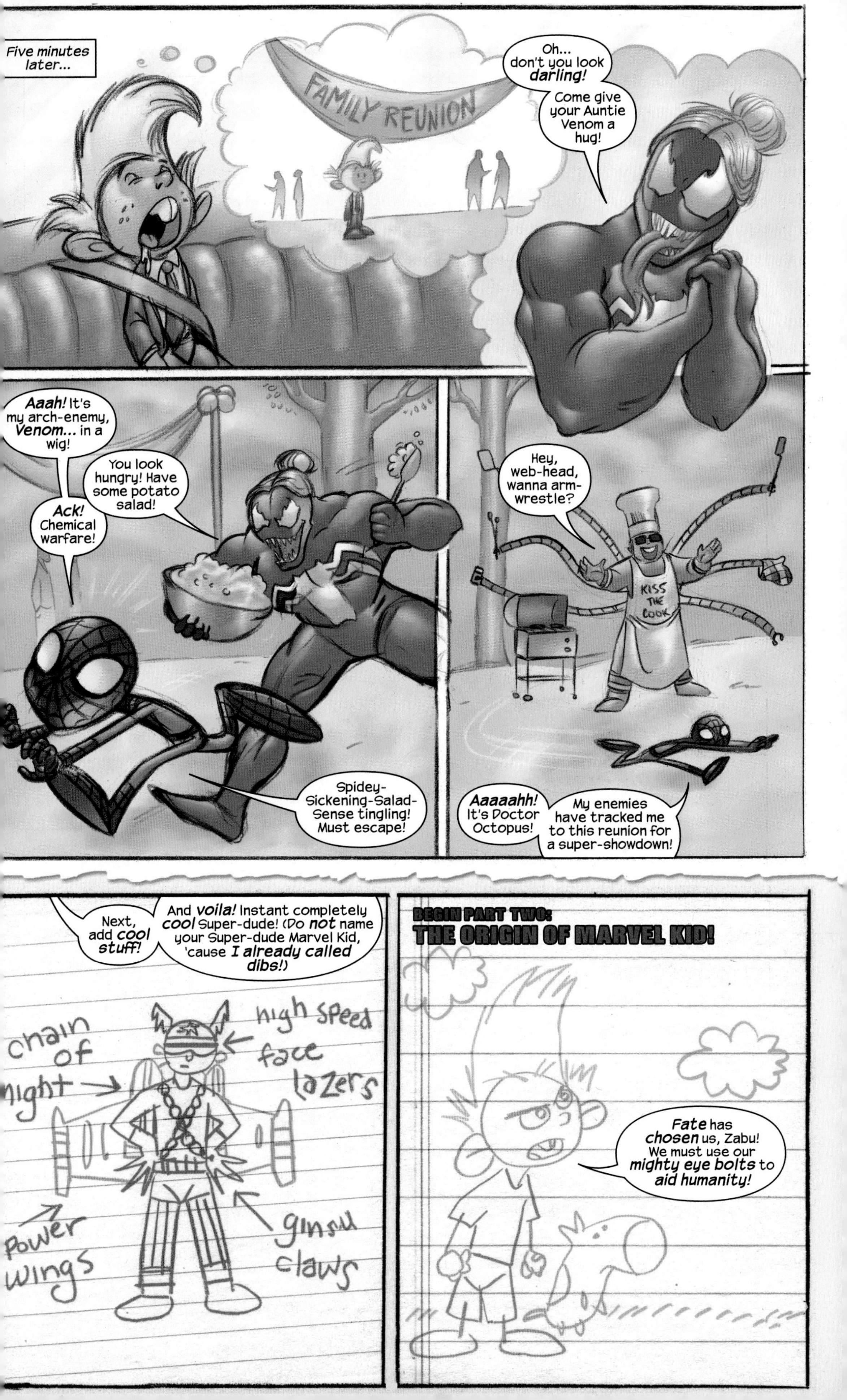

Five minutes later...
FAMILY REUNION
Oh... don't you look darling!
Come give your Auntie Venom a hug!
Aaah! It's my arch-enemy, Venom... in a wig!
You look hungry! Have some potato salad!
Ack! Chemical warfare!
Spidey-Sickening-Salad-Sense tingling! Must escape!
Hey, web-head, wanna arm-wrestle?
KISS THE COOK
Aaaaahh! It's Doctor Octopus!
My enemies have tracked me to this reunion for a super-showdown!
Next, add cool stuff!
And voila! Instant completely cool Super-dude! (Do not name your Super-dude Marvel Kid, 'cause I already called dibs!)
chain of might
high speed face lazers
power wings
ginsu claws
BEGIN PART TWO:
THE ORIGIN OF MARVEL KID!
Fate has chosen us, Zabu! We must use our mighty eye bolts to aid humanity!

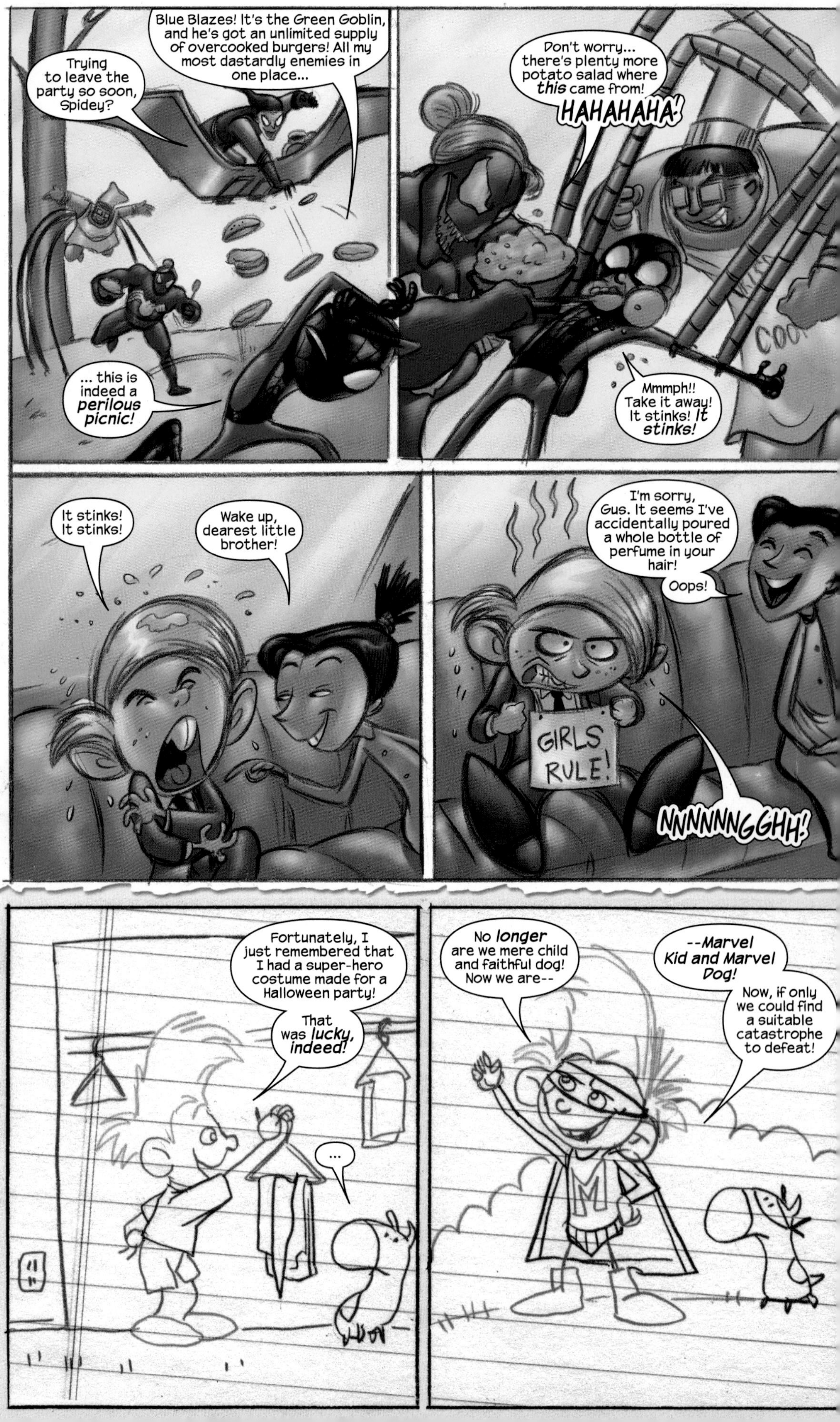
Trying to leave the party so soon, Spidey?
Blue Blazes! It's the Green Goblin, and he's got an unlimited supply of overcooked burgers! All my most dastardly enemies in one place...
... this is indeed a *perilous picnic!*
Don't worry... there's plenty more potato salad where *this* came from!
HAHAHAHA!
Mmmph!! Take it away! It stinks! *It stinks!*
It stinks! It stinks!
Wake up, dearest little brother!
I'm sorry, Gus. It seems I've accidentally poured a whole bottle of perfume in your hair!
Oops!
GIRLS RULE!
NNNNNNGGHH!
Fortunately, I just remembered that I had a super-hero costume made for a Halloween party!
That was *lucky, indeed!*
...
No *longer* are we mere child and faithful dog! Now we are--
--*Marvel Kid and Marvel Dog!*
Now, if only we could find a suitable catastrophe to defeat!

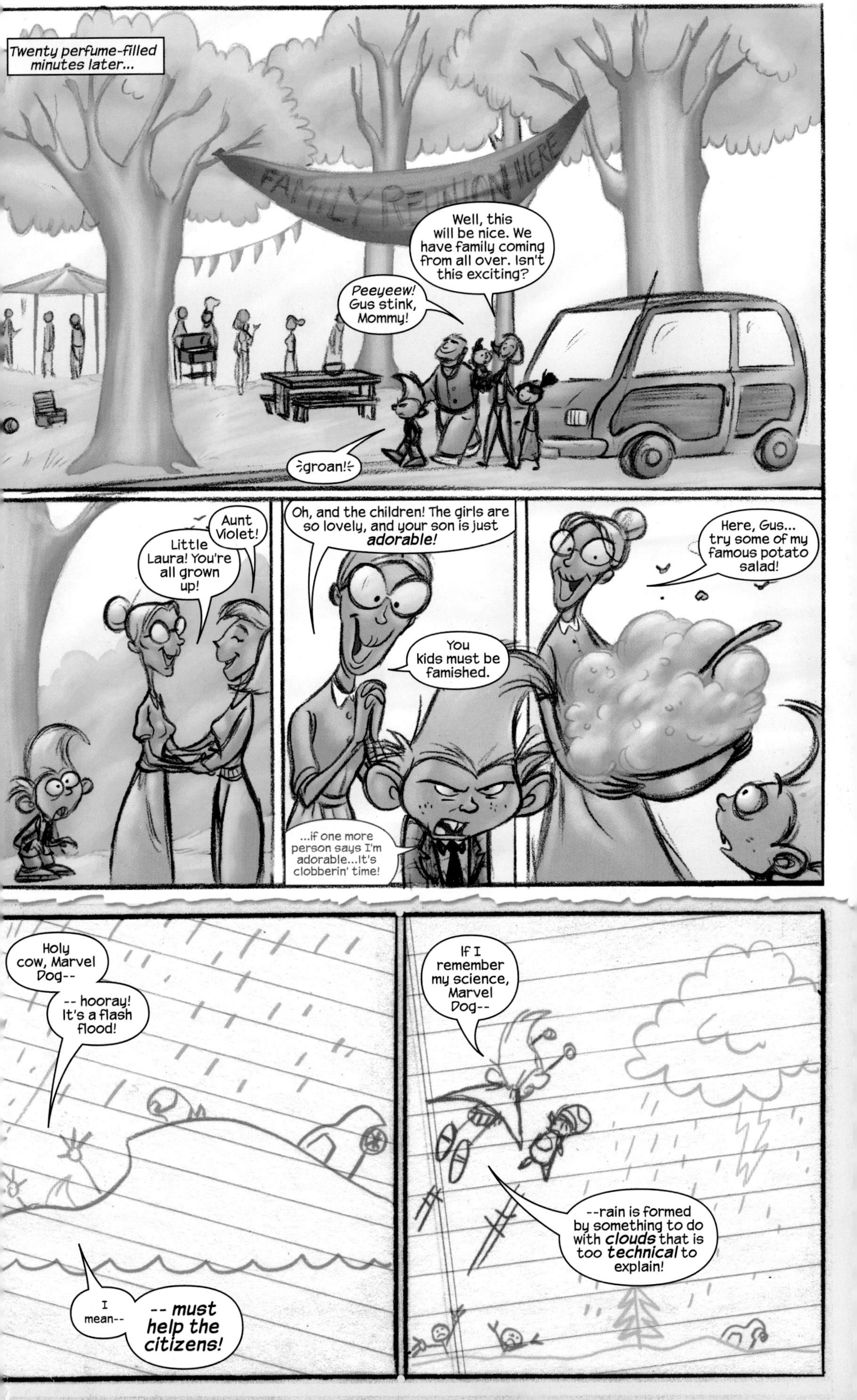
Twenty perfume-filled minutes later...
FAMILY REUNION HERE
Well, this will be nice. We have family coming from all over. Isn't this exciting?
Peeyeew! Gus stink, Mommy!
groan!
Aunt Violet!
Little Laura! You're all grown up!
Oh, and the children! The girls are so lovely, and your son is just adorable!
You kids must be famished.
...if one more person says I'm adorable...It's clobberin' time!
Here, Gus... try some of my famous potato salad!
Holy cow, Marvel Dog--
-- hooray! It's a flash flood!
I mean--
-- must help the citizens!
If I remember my science, Marvel Dog--
--rain is formed by something to do with clouds that is too technical to explain!

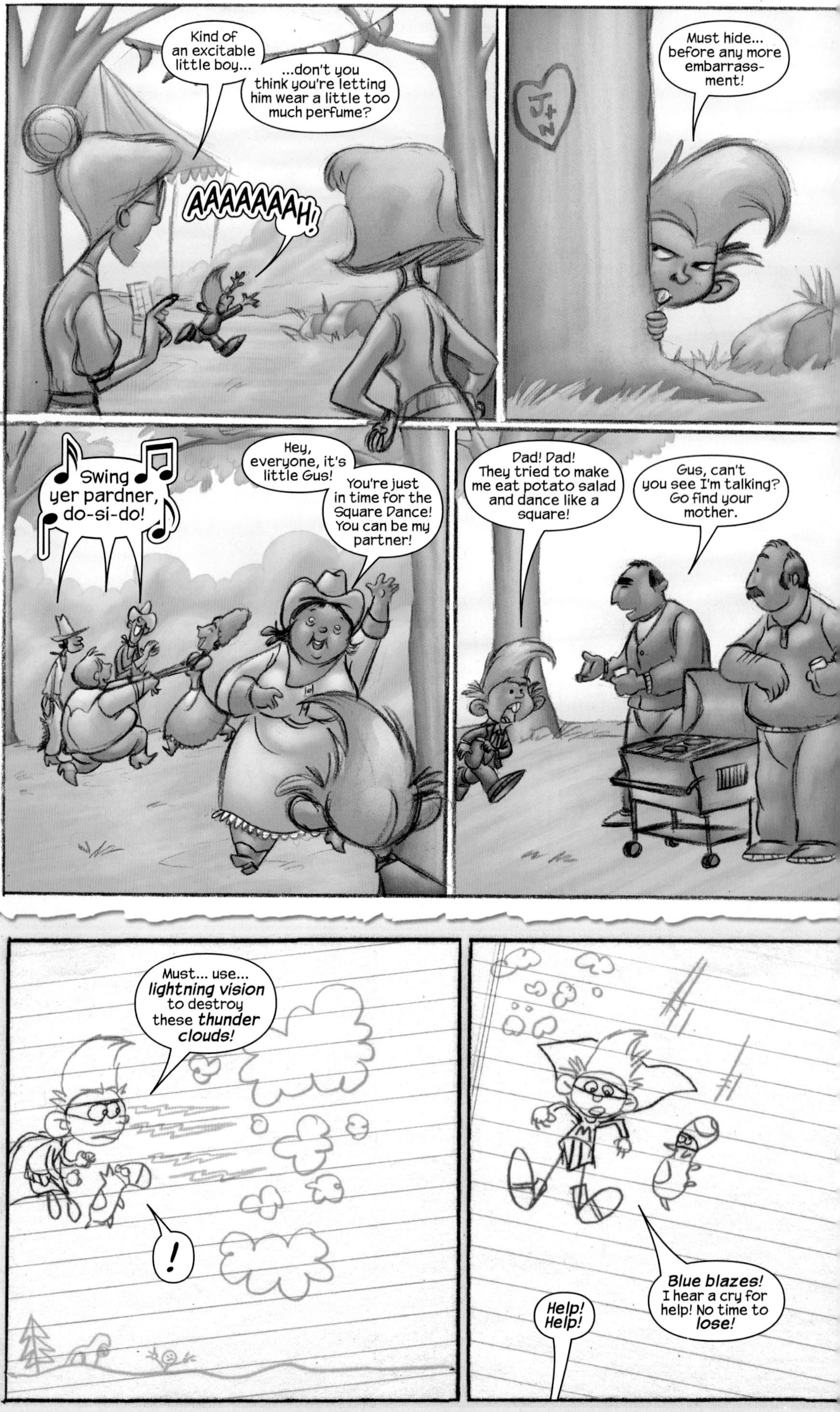

Kind of an excitable little boy...
...don't you think you're letting him wear a little too much perfume?
AAAAAAAH!
Must hide... before any more embarrass-ment!
Swing yer pardner, do-si-do!
Hey, everyone, it's little Gus!
You're just in time for the Square Dance! You can be my partner!
Dad! Dad! They tried to make me eat potato salad and dance like a square!
Gus, can't you see I'm talking? Go find your mother.
Must... use... *lightning vision* to destroy these *thunder clouds!*
!
Help! Help!
Blue blazes! I hear a cry for help! No time to *lose!*

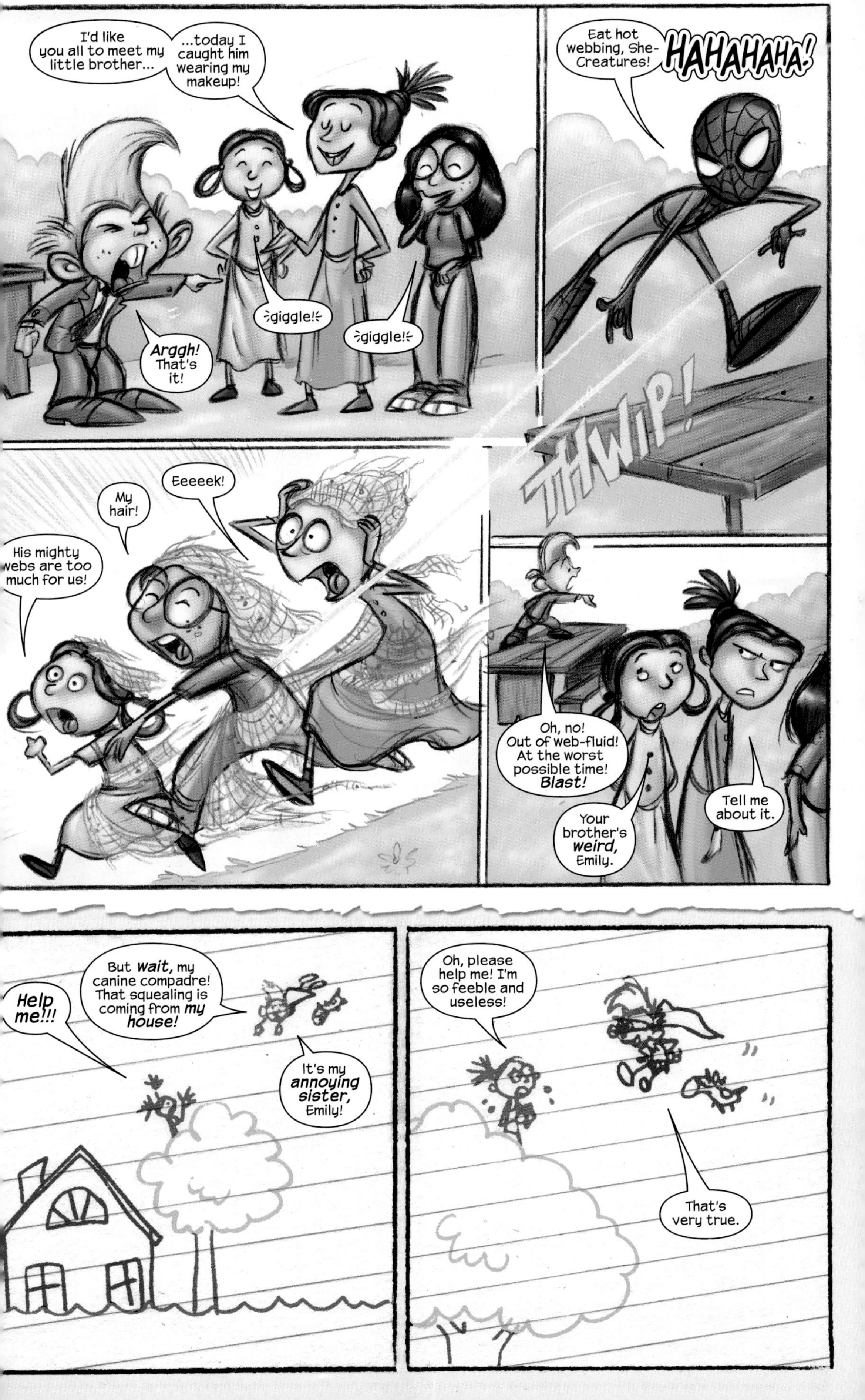

I'd like you all to meet my little brother...
...today I caught him wearing my makeup!
Arggh! That's it!
giggle!
giggle!
Eat hot webbing, She-Creatures!
HAHAHAHA!
THWIP!
His mighty webs are too much for us!
My hair!
Eeeeek!
Oh, no! Out of web-fluid! At the worst possible time! Blast!
Your brother's weird, Emily.
Tell me about it.
Help me!!!
But wait, my canine compadre! That squealing is coming from my house!
It's my annoying sister, Emily!
Oh, please help me! I'm so feeble and useless!
That's very true.

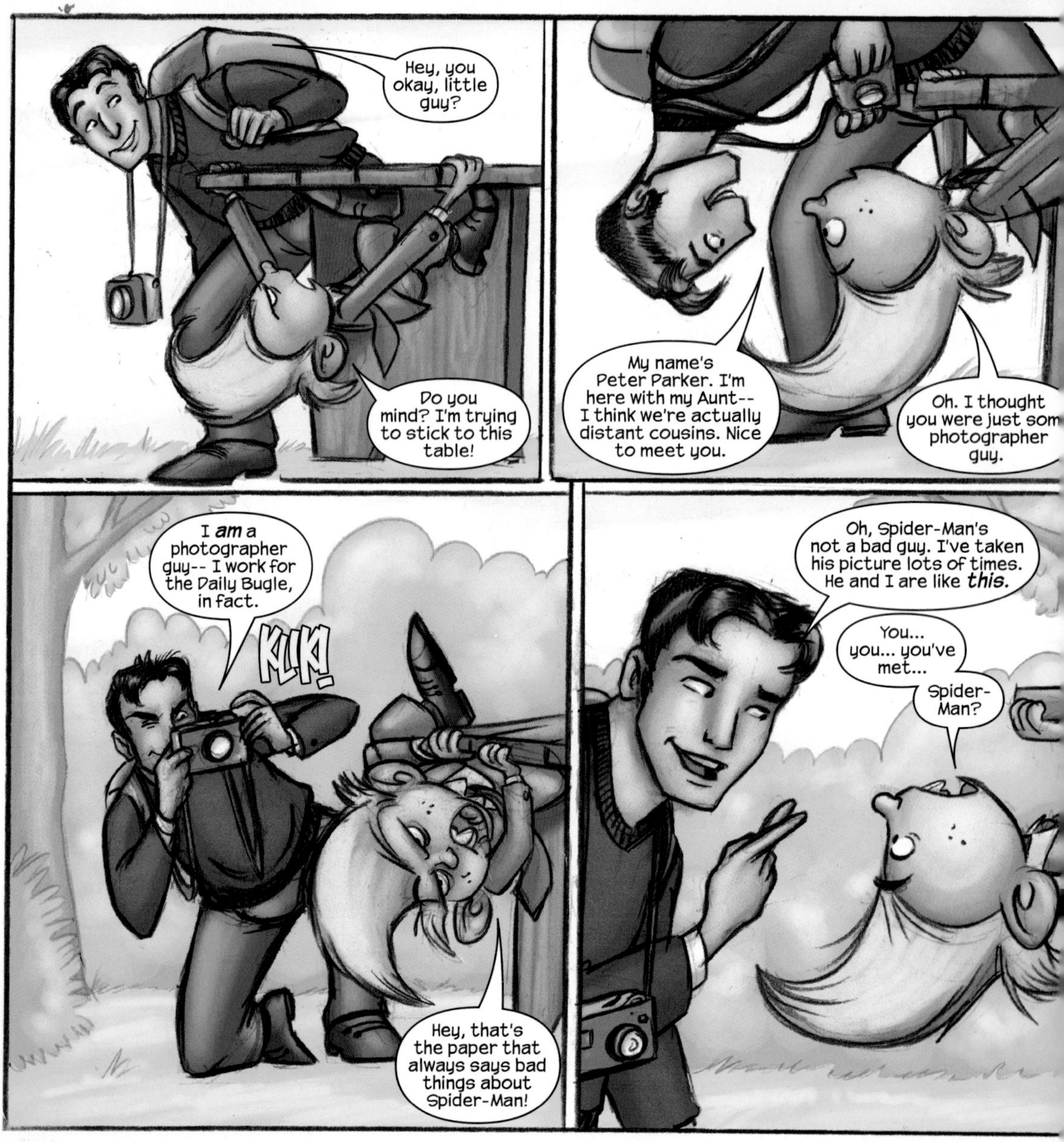

Hey, you okay, little guy?
Do you mind? I'm trying to stick to this table!
My name's Peter Parker. I'm here with my Aunt-- I think we're actually distant cousins. Nice to meet you.
Oh. I thought you were just som photographer guy.
I *am* a photographer guy-- I work for the Daily Bugle, in fact.
KLIK!
Hey, that's the paper that always says bad things about Spider-Man!
Oh, Spider-Man's not a bad guy. I've taken his picture lots of times. He and I are like *this.*
You... you... you've met...
Spider-Man?

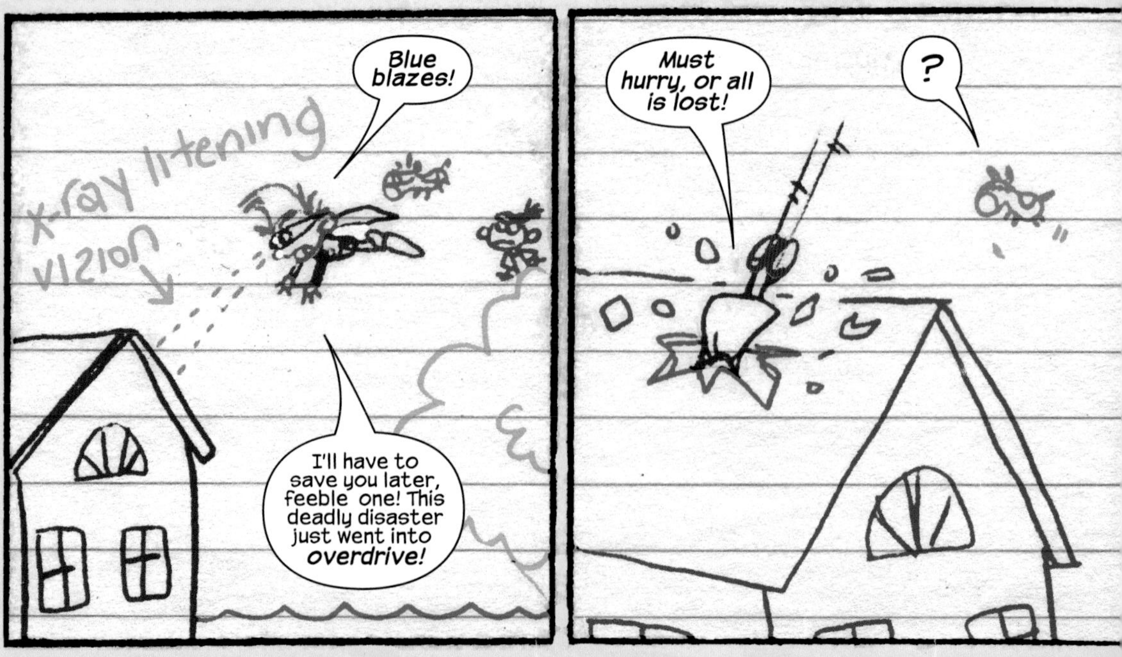

Blue blazes!
x-ray litening
vizion
I'll have to save you later, feeble one! This deadly disaster just went into *overdrive!*
Must hurry, or all is lost!
?

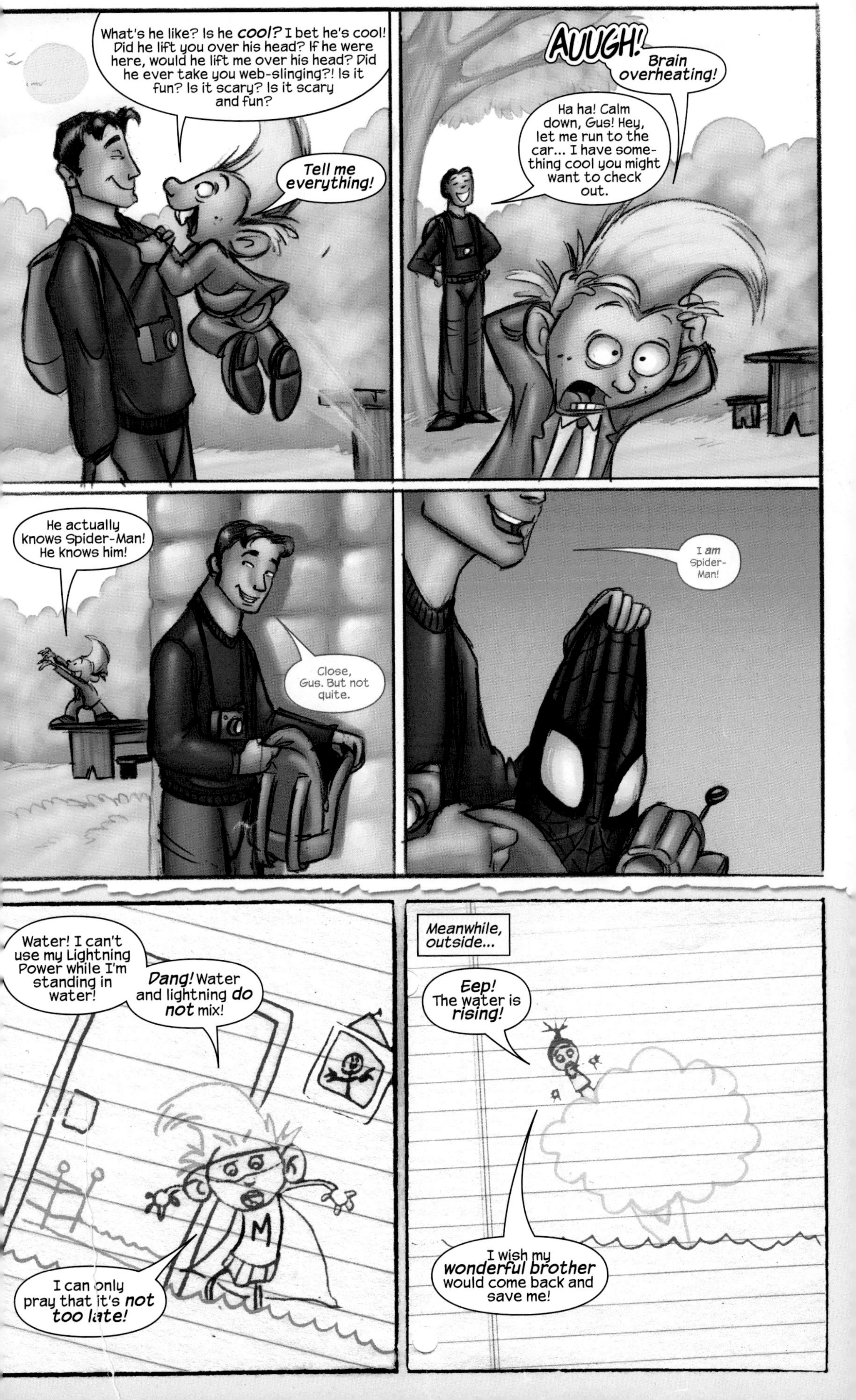

What's he like? Is he cool? I bet he's cool! Did he lift you over his head? If he were here, would he lift me over his head? Did he ever take you web-slinging?! Is it fun? Is it scary? Is it scary and fun?
Tell me everything!
AUUGH!
Brain overheating!
Ha ha! Calm down, Gus! Hey, let me run to the car... I have something cool you might want to check out.
He actually knows Spider-Man! He knows him!
Close, Gus. But not quite.
I am Spider-Man!
Water! I can't use my Lightning Power while I'm standing in water!
Dang! Water and lightning do not mix!
I can only pray that it's not too late!
Meanwhile, outside...
Eep! The water is rising!
I wish my wonderful brother would come back and save me!

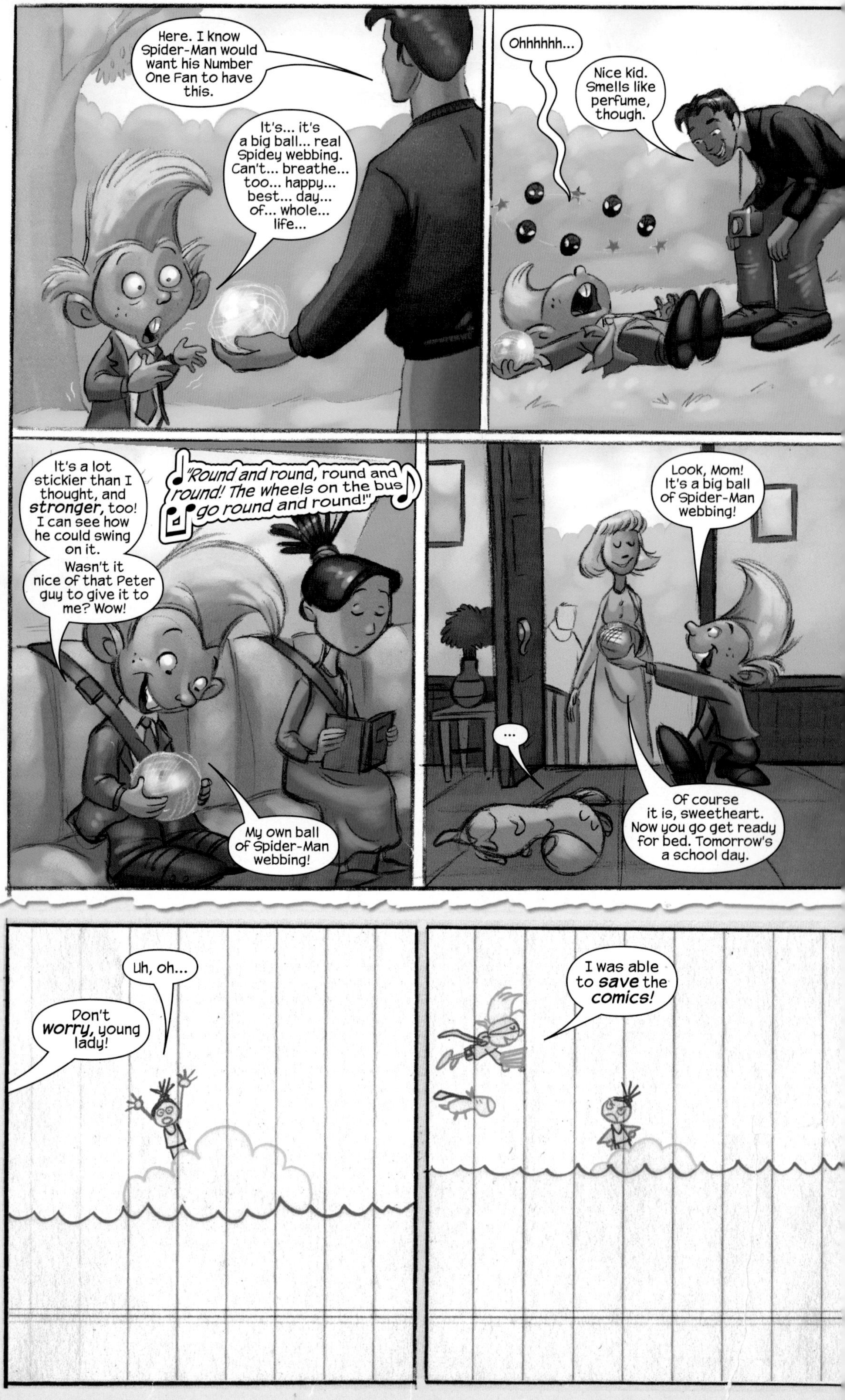

Here. I know Spider-Man would want his Number One Fan to have this.
It's... it's a big ball... real Spidey webbing. Can't... breathe... too... happy... best... day... of... whole... life...
Ohhhhhh...
Nice kid. Smells like perfume, though.
It's a lot stickier than I thought, and stronger, too! I can see how he could swing on it.
"Round and round, round and round! The wheels on the bus go round and round!"
Wasn't it nice of that Peter guy to give it to me? Wow!
My own ball of Spider-Man webbing!
Look, Mom! It's a big ball of Spider-Man webbing!
...
Of course it is, sweetheart. Now you go get ready for bed. Tomorrow's a school day.
Uh, oh...
Don't worry, young lady!
I was able to save the comics!

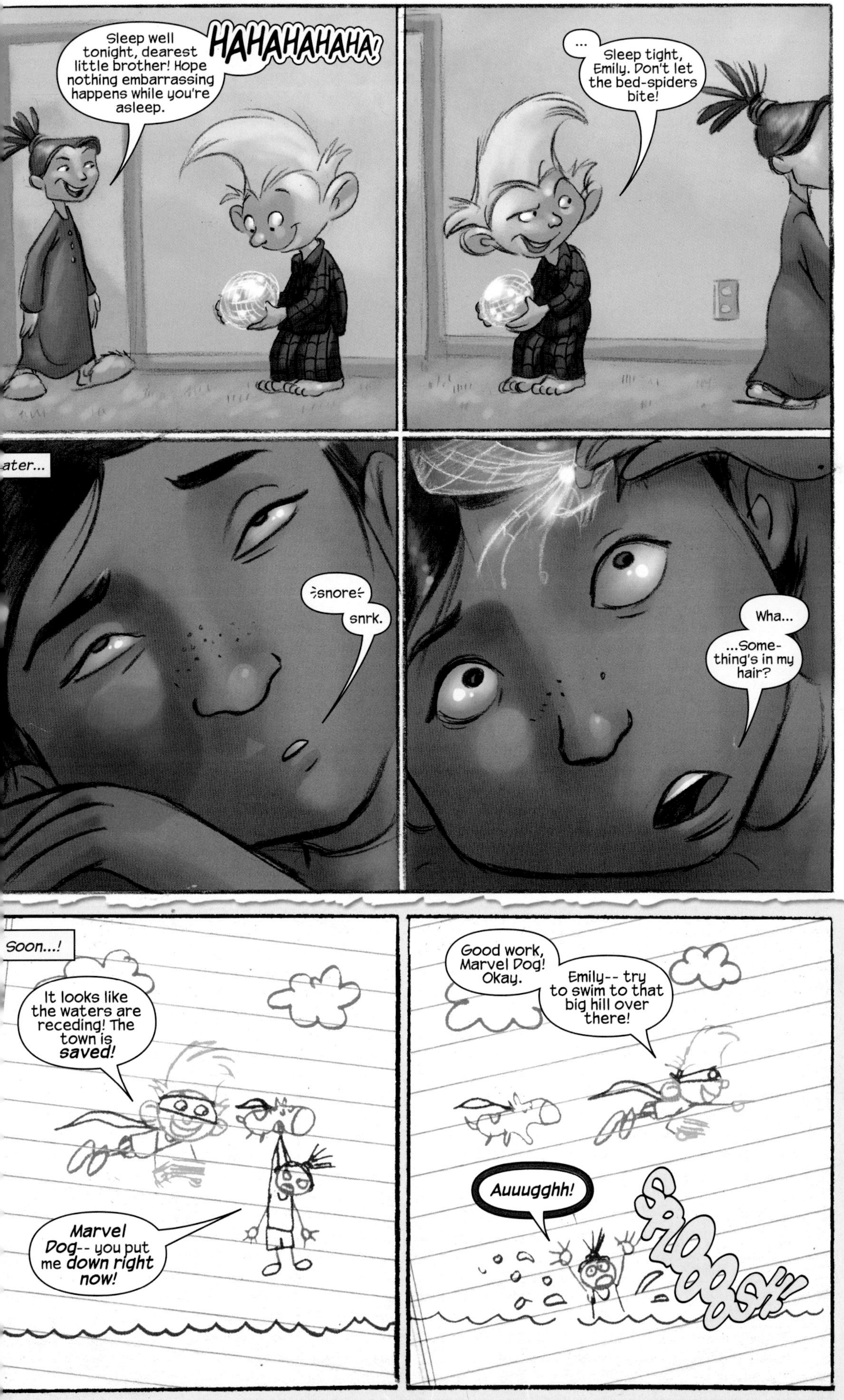
Sleep well tonight, dearest little brother! Hope nothing embarrassing happens while you're asleep.
HAHAHAHAHA!
...
Sleep tight, Emily. Don't let the bed-spiders bite!
ater...
snore
snrk.
Wha...
...Some-thing's in my hair?
Soon...!
It looks like the waters are receding! The town is saved!
Marvel Dog-- you put me down right now!
Good work, Marvel Dog! Okay.
Emily-- try to swim to that big hill over there!
Auuugghh!
SPLOOOSH!

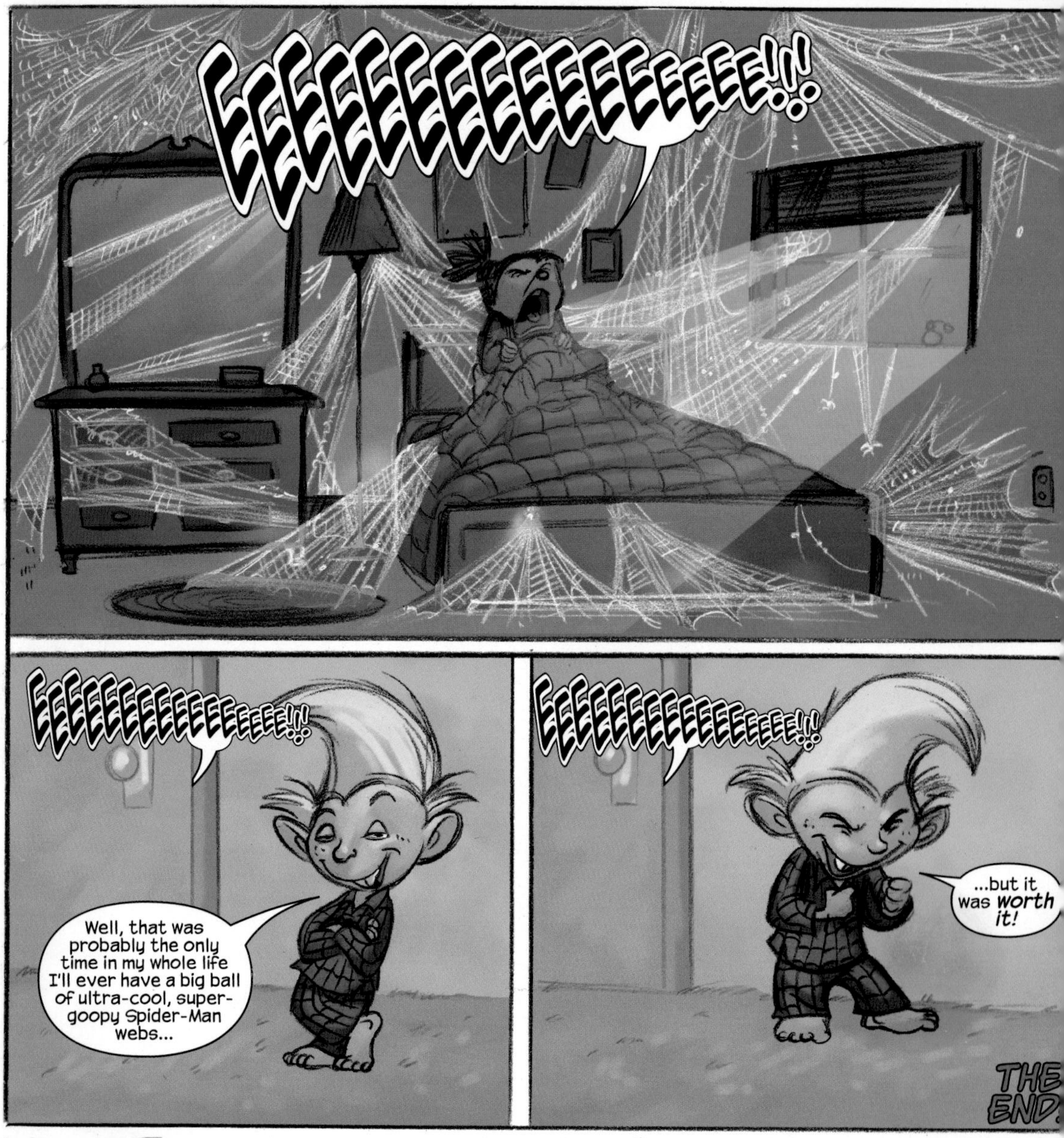
EEEEEEEEEEEEEEEEEE!!!
EEEEEEEEEEEEEEEEE!!!
Well, that was probably the only time in my whole life I'll ever have a big ball of ultra-cool, super-goopy Spider-Man webs...
EEEEEEEEEEEEEEEEE!!!
...but it was *worth it!*
THE END.

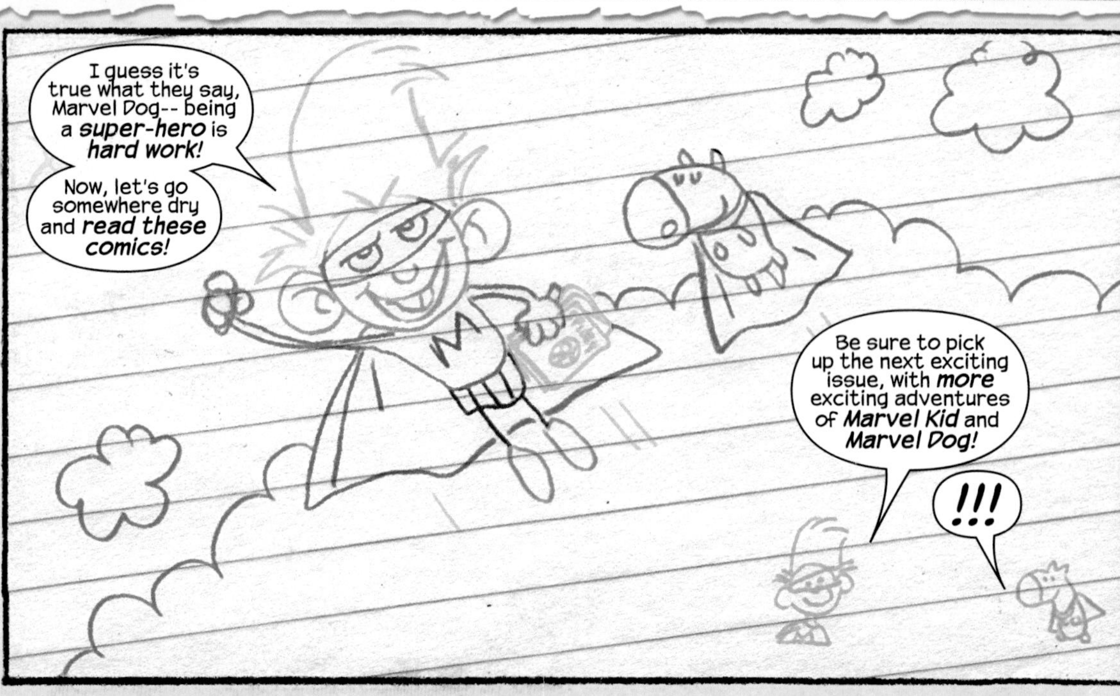
I guess it's true what they say, Marvel Dog-- being a *super-hero* is *hard work!*
Now, let's go somewhere dry and *read these comics!*
Be sure to pick up the next exciting issue, with *more* exciting adventures of *Marvel Kid* and *Marvel Dog!*
!!!